FEARFUL SYMMETRY

Also by Lilla M. Waltch

THE THIRD VICTIM

FEARFUL SYMMETRY

Lilla M. Waltch

Dodd, Mead & Company
New York

For Mark

Published by Dodd, Mead & Company, Inc.
71 Fifth Avenue, New York, NY 10003
Manufactured in the United States of America

First Edition

1   2   3   4   5   6   7   8   9   10

Library of Congress Cataloging-in-Publication Data

Waltch, Lilla M.
  Fearful symmetry.
  I. Title.
PS3573.A47227F4   1988   813'.54   87-33187
ISBN 0-396-09348-5

1

Lisa Davis sat on a folding chair in the main exhibit room of the Braeton Zoo's new Primates Building. She checked the program in her lap. Speeches first: Mr. John Winston, President of the Braeton Zoological Society; Mr. Matthew Yates, Director of the Braeton Zoo; and Mrs. John Winston, Director of Development for the Braeton Zoo. Then dinner and dancing. The bar set up near the lobby doors had been doing a brisk business when she arrived, but now everyone was seated in front of the speakers' platform that stood near the largest cage. The cage was empty, as were all the other cages. Lisa sipped her ginger ale. The people sitting in the rows of chairs were dressed in tuxedos and evening gowns. They chatted with one another and drank from plastic cups.

When the clapping started, Lisa turned her head toward the back of the room, and she saw him. Matt Yates. He entered through the lobby doors and walked down the aisle between the rows of chairs with another man and a woman. She hadn't seen Matt since she was fifteen years old, but she would have recognized him anywhere. He smiled nervously and looked down at the floor, running his fingers through his thick brown hair, just as he used to do whenever he felt ill at ease. The tuxedo did nothing to disguise his awkward-

1

ness. Lisa guessed he'd rented it for the occasion and that he'd probably never worn one before.

Matt and the other man waited while the woman stepped up the few stairs onto the platform. Lisa leaned forward in her seat to get a better view of her. She had the kind of looks you wanted to lean forward to see. She must have been six feet tall with flowing black hair. She wore a bright red dress, which she lifted up at the hem to climb the steps. On her feet were sandals made of silver sequins. Lisa looked at her program again. Mrs. John Winston, obviously. Mrs. Winston walked across the platform and sat in one of the folding chairs. Matt Yates sat beside her.

The other man, who must be Mr. Winston, went straight to the podium. Lisa knelt in the aisle and snapped his picture as he smiled into the applauding audience. When he began to speak, she returned to her seat. In the tone of a proud father bragging about his child's achievements, John Winston told of the growth of the zoo and its increasing fiscal soundness since he became president of the Braeton Zoological Society. Lisa scribbled furiously, trying to get it all down. After a while she noticed that every sentence began with "I" and she stopped trying so hard. He reminded her of someone. She couldn't think who.

Matt Yates looked out at the well-dressed descendants of the primates who would soon inhabit this space. They were listening attentively to John Winston as he welcomed them to the Gala. John could be charming. Tall and lean with a big voice, he knew how to tell his stories of animal hunts and zoo successes in a way that grabbed the interest of the crowd and he knew how to make them laugh. Matt observed the eager, amused faces and sighed. Unfortunately, John never bothered to use his charm on him. John hadn't been enthusiastic about Matt's taking over the directorship of the zoo. He made Matt feel as if he were constantly on trial, an extremely unpleasant feeling.

Matt looked at Jacky Winston next to him. She was staring straight ahead, beyond the crowd, her face quiet, unreadable. Matt wondered about her, what she was thinking as her husband rode the crest of his ego trip. In the first row Johnny Winston was drinking steadily. Matt wished he could tell the young man to wipe that look of disgust off his face as he watched his father. But maybe Johnny didn't care who knew how he felt. Matt scanned the crowd to see if Alden Vining had made it to the Gala. He was supposed to give the treasurer's report tonight, but he'd been ill. Matt couldn't see him anywhere.

Suddenly everyone was clapping again and looking toward him. John was motioning to him. Matt got to his feet. Trying to smile, he made his way to the podium, aware that his rented trousers were too short and he'd forgotten to polish his shoes.

He stood at the podium for a few moments, his heart pounding. Then he slid uncomfortably into the speech as if it were a tepid bath. "Thank you for coming and thank you for your help in building this much needed home for our primates." He looked out at the faces and experienced a wave of stage fright. He took a sip of water. When he looked up again, he'd forgotten his speech. Closing his eyes for a moment, he pictured Pansy, the zoo's beautiful lowland gorilla, her intelligent face peering into her newborn baby's eyes, her massive arms cradling the infant, and the words came. "As you know, Pansy, our gorilla, has recently made us all as proud as grandparents. Pansy and Lily, plus our other great apes and smaller primates, will move into these new quarters next week."

Matt relaxed a little as his prepared speech came back to

3

him. "I think you are all aware of our commitment to breeding animals in the zoo, especially those of endangered species that may soon be extinct in their natural habitats. To do so we need space, expert advice, and healthy animals. Through your generous support we are moving along in this very important program. Several new babies have been born this year, and Anuk, our female polar bear, gave birth to two healthy cubs last winter. But I needn't enumerate all our breeding successes. You have only to take a tour around the zoo to see for yourselves what your generosity has made possible."

Matt breathed a sigh of relief and took another sip of water. It was almost over. "Thank you again for coming here tonight and for helping to make our dreams a reality, a reality from which you and your children and your children's children will benefit.

"And thanks to Jacky Winston who produced this event and who recently produced another event, the acquisition of a pair of Brazilian jaguars that arrived here last week and are in their new quarters at the Big Cats House. It is our hope that we can make our new jaguars feel comfortable enough here so that they, too, will add to our zoo population. And now I leave you in the most capable of hands, Jacky Winston."

They were clapping again as he left the podium. A camera light flashed. Matt passed beside Jacky and she kissed him on the cheek. He felt her cool lips and smelled her cinnamony perfume. Johnny Winston was leaning back in his seat, tie loosened. He flicked an amused eyebrow as he met Matt's eye.

"You're a great bunch," Jacky began. "Look what you've done." Her arms were spread wide as if to encompass the whole building of concrete, glass, and steel. Her voice was husky with feeling. Her love of the place is so deep it touches

4

them all, Matt thought as he sat down. He felt the sweat trickling down his face. His shirt was soaked. He sat back, taking big gulping breaths.

———————

Lisa also felt relief as Matt sat down. He hasn't changed a bit, she thought. He'd rather face an enraged lion than a roomful of people. She turned her attention to Jacky Winston, who had no such problem. She was describing the capture of a pair of jaguars in the jungles of Brazil.

Lisa prepared her camera for the next shot as she listened. So far her job as a reporter for the Braeton *Times* had been humdrum. What could you expect of a weekly newspaper in a small university town outside of Boston? Still, she felt excited to be here, lucky to have been assigned to this story. She'd always loved zoos. One of the few memories she had of her father was of going to the Franklin Park Zoo with him. She remembered his hand enveloping hers, the calluses on his palms. Standing together in the smelly Elephant House watching the huge beasts picking up hay with their trunks, he'd told her elephants were wise and she'd always believed it.

Now Mrs. Winston seemed to be winding up her talk. Lisa slipped her notepad into her pocketbook and slid out of her seat. Crouching in the aisle, she adjusted her camera and snapped. That would be a good one, she thought. Mrs. Winston looked so vibrant, Lisa wished she were taking color shots instead of black-and-white.

As soon as the speeches were over, the audience got up and moved back to the bar. At first Lisa followed Matt, trying to get close enough for a word with him, but he was surrounded by people. She was going to meet with him tomorrow morning anyway. She'd called his secretary and made an appointment to interview him for her article.

Lisa snapped another picture of him. The expression on his face was one of such longing that Lisa followed his gaze. There could be no mistake about whom he was watching. His eyes never left the beautiful woman in red as she stood with her husband at the bar. Lisa pressed the shutter although she felt uneasy about capturing his expression on film. In the sudden flash of light, Matt turned his head toward her. Now was her chance to talk to him, but the lingering expression on his face made her uncomfortable. She'd wait until tomorrow.

Matt caught a glimpse of a dark-haired young woman as the strobe light flashed in his face. There was something about her, something familiar. She must be the reporter from the Braeton *Times*. Had he met her before? He started to say hello, but she was already moving away. He turned back to the bar. The tuxedoed men getting drinks looked like white-faced penguins jostling for position at the fish trough. Jacky was in the center of the group. She threw her head back and laughed. At the base of her long curved throat diamonds sparkled. She looked like a bird of paradise. Her black hair fell straight and silky on either side of her high forehead. Her facial structure was a little too pronounced for beauty: high cheekbones, slightly protruding jaw, and a nose that curved gently downward, giving her an aggressive, predatory appearance. More falcon than bird of paradise, he thought. She was tall, taller than her husband who stood next to her, and she had the supple body of an athletic woman. The red chiffon strapless gown accentuated the whiteness of her skin.

He wanted to go over to her, just to stand next to her, hear her voice, smell her perfume, but people were talking to him and asking him questions. When he was finally able to excuse himself, Jacky and John, now standing apart from the others, seemed to be in the midst of a whispered argument. Matt went over to the hors d'oeuvres table where he ate shrimp and talked to Stan Clayburgh and his wife Fran.

2

"BITCH," John Winston said as they left the Primates Building. He squeezed Jacky's forearm.

She breathed in sharply. "Take your hand off."

A departing guest turned at the sound of her voice.

"Good night, Harry," John said. "Thanks again." He loosened his grip on Jacky's arm, but steered her toward his white Saab parked at the curb. "Get in," he ordered.

"We'll talk right here." Jacky rubbed her arm where he'd hurt her and pulled her red chiffon scarf across her shoulders. The night was getting chilly.

"The remarks you made to Fran Clayburgh about Mariel and me were uncalled for."

Jacky sighed. She looked up at the sky, hoping to see a falling star she could wish on. It was the season, but no such luck. "I'm supposed to be deaf, dumb, and blind, is that it?"

He reached for her again. She stepped back. He let his arms fall to his sides. "Look, Jacky, I thought we had an arrangement."

"News to me." She looked up at the sky again.

"You want to discuss this, is that what you're telling me?"

"I'm not stupid."

8

He sighed, exasperated. "You want this spelled out? Now, after all these years?"

"Maybe I'm just sick of being your patsy. Nice, tactful little Jacky, who looks the other way while John, pillar of the community, plays around with any available whore."

"You will not talk that way about Mariel."

"I'm sick of the phoniness of all this." She gestured toward the newly finished building.

"What do you want? You think we could get it back, what we used to have?" He wasn't being sarcastic.

She didn't answer. She looked down at the gravel path. He'd never give her what she wanted. She knew better than to ask.

Now his voice was soft, placating. "I thought everything was all right, Jacky. We loved each other once. We've been good to each other. I thought you had what you wanted now. I do."

Still she said nothing.

"You have the breeding farm, all the big game hunts you want. Everything money can buy. And I haven't been bad to you. Mariel's taken nothing you wanted."

He was right. Mariel had taken nothing she wanted. "I want my freedom."

He waved his arm magnanimously. "You have but to ask."

He was smiling. The bastard was actually smiling. "And I'd get a kiss good-bye."

"You agreed," he said, pained.

"I agreed. Goodnight, John." She walked away from the car door he was holding open for her, her high heels wobbling on the loose gravel of the walk. After a few moments she heard the car door slam and the sound of the engine starting up. She didn't look back.

Unlike him to drive off like that, Jacky thought, as she

9

walked back toward the Primates Building where she could either pick up a ride or call a cab. John was usually careful about appearances, trusting her to fill in any gaps in his image of attentive husband. Maybe this is a good sign. Maybe he's really in love with Mariel. If he left me, I wouldn't have any worries. . . . A sleek black car stopped beside her.

Stan Clayburgh opened the window. "Anything wrong, Jacky?"

She looked past his shoulder at Fran's inquisitive face and smiled. "Left my lipstick in the ladies'."

Jacky walked on. After all, John had divorced Charlotte to marry her, she thought, stepping back onto the grass as another car went by. And when he left Charlotte, he'd left a big chunk of his fortune with her. That was why, he'd explained to Jacky when they decided to get married, she must sign a prenuptial agreement. He couldn't take any more chances with his estate. It wasn't fair to his kids— to John Jr., who hadn't found himself yet, and Abigail with her large family in Greenwich. The agreement had seemed fair to her at the time. If she left him, she would get nothing. If he left her, however, she would receive a generous settlement.

She'd been too young to understand what she was doing. In love for the first time in her life at twenty-six, she'd thought it would last forever. John at forty-six had seemed kind and good, beset with family problems, needing her desperately. Only later had she discovered some of the realities beneath his attractive surface. She had learned something about his egomania and how it related to his attitude toward money. He would buy his wife every luxury. He would give millions to charity and to the zoo, but he wouldn't allow one penny to be taken from him without his willing it, not to mention a wife.

10

A long low car stopped suddenly in a spray of gravel beside her. "Get in, Mommy," said the voice, soft with a mocking edge to it.

"Johnny. Just the person I want to see." She ran around the front of the car and got in.

He took off fast. The windows open. The cold night air whipped her long black hair across her face. She laughed. "What timing."

"Where to, Mommy?"

"What's that pitch-dark bar of yours that makes the heavenly scotch sours?"

"Touch of Sin."

"Sounds about right."

"Why did you want to see me?" Instantly suspicious, as was his nature, but why shouldn't he be? He hadn't had it easy. His mother, John's first wife Libby, hadn't landed a chunk of John's fortune as Charlotte had. She'd totaled her silver Cadillac and herself when Johnny was six. Luckily she'd been alone. She'd been drunk, very drunk, the medical examiner said after they'd managed to extricate her from the car with the jaws of life.

"Better be nice to me," Johnny often told Jacky. "You're the closest I'll ever come to having a mother." Their joke. She was six years older than he.

They drove to the Braeton Arms. A Touch of Sin was on the first floor of the hotel, classy, art deco with shiny black laminated surfaces and accents of pink you could barely see in the candlelight. Jacky and Johnny sank into a dark sofa and were served a pitcher of scotch sours. The waiters wore black. They were nearly invisible.

Johnny took Jacky's hand and played with her fingers on

the shiny table top. "I love going out with you. You are one beautiful woman. No one'd ever guess that I wasn't straight or that you were my mommy."

"Thanks, Sonny," Jacky said dryly, "but who could even see me in here?" She felt a buzz as she swallowed the strong drink. It burnt a path down her throat, warmed her stomach. She leaned toward Johnny. "I really care about you." He pretended to ogle her cleavage. They both laughed.

His glass was empty. He poured another, filled hers almost to the top. "I know you care, Mommy. And I know why."

"Does there have to be a why?" Jacky picked up her drink carefully but some of it sloshed over the sides anyway. She took a big sip and put it down. Johnny was looking at her intently. "Okay, so why," she said at last. She held the candle close to his face. His eyes like his father's, set far apart, large and blue, gave him a look of openness, but you had to look way into them, Jacky thought, to find any truth at all. She sighed, put the candle down. It was too dark in here.

"Because we're fellow victims. We're flies trapped by the same spider."

"Nice metaphor. But not really accurate." She held a maraschino cherry by the stem and bit into it.

"What do you mean, not accurate?"

"You want to get away. But you're too dependent on him, and not just because of money."

Johnny nodded. "You loved him too, didn't you? Once?"

"Oh, yes." Jacky breathed out slowly.

"He still cares about you. He told me. He said you're friends."

Friends? She thought about it. She knew John admired her still, that he even liked her and liked to be with her. He'd made the rules. She'd followed them—for a long time. She tapped a fingernail against her cold glass. "Friends of a sort," she admitted. It had been all right for a long time. It wasn't anymore.

"You're in love with someone," he said.

She started.

"I know you well enough so I can see through your good manners."

"I'm sorry. I would've told you, but secrecy seemed important."

"Sure. He'd cut you off if he knew."

His stating it so plainly made her feel like a moneygrubber. Well, she was. She didn't want to give it all up. Why should she? "But you're not trapped, like me," she said partly to change the subject.

He laughed, a bleak sound. "I'm not?" He grabbed her hand again and even in the dark, she could see the intensity of his eyes. "I love Koo," he whispered.

"And he?" she asked.

He heard it in her voice. "I know you don't think much of him. But you're wrong. He's a wonderful person. He's had a horrible life. That's what makes him act the way he does. Underneath he's kind and caring. He loves me, Jacky. He'll make me happy. I need him."

Jacky weighed what she should say, how far she should go toward telling him what he didn't want to hear. Even through the bubbly feeling in her head, she knew she should be careful. "Why are you trapped because of your love for Koo? Why can't you just go on the way you've been?"

"Because I want things to be different," he said in that petulant voice that so antagonized his father. "I want this to be it." He quieted, looked down at the table. "He wants to move in with me. He wants . . . we both want a commitment."

Jacky started to say something.

He held up a hand. "No. Let me finish. I've wanted to

13

tell you." He picked up her hand again. "Please, Jacky. Please. You're the only one I can talk to."

Jacky pressed his hand. She felt sorrow for him, and longed to help. It would be a mistake to let Koo move into his opulent apartment. John would be furious. Johnny was such a push-over for love, his need so great, he'd walk straight into disaster.

"So," he continued, "as you know, when Koo moves in, it'll all be out in the open. Dad will know." He gave a little laugh. "He's never been quite sure about me and now he'll see that, just as he feared, I'm a queer. And you know Dad, I'll be out on my ass."

"That's why I think . . ."

"What I'm telling you is I don't give a fuck. . . ."

The black-suited waiter was approaching.

"Another pitcher," Johnny said.

"He'll never allow it," Jacky said. "He'll be ashamed, for all his friends."

"I have a little money."

Jacky nodded. His mother had managed to scrape together a trust fund before she died. It would keep him alive. Not much more. Johnny was used to luxury. If John cut him off, there wouldn't be any. She thought she knew how Koo would feel about that. "Koo . . ." she started to say.

"Koo loves me, not my money," Johnny said.

Maybe it was the alcohol befogging her brain or maybe just impatience, Jacky couldn't help herself. "He's not what you think. I know. Trust me."

Johnny took his hand away from hers and stood up, nearly tipping over the pitcher the waiter was sliding onto the table. "You're just like all the rest. You think you know it all. You don't care how I feel," he said, his voice childish. "Trust you." He laughed. He turned to the waiter who was listening and shoved some bills at him. "Here. And get the lady a taxi." He walked away.

14

Jacky half rose, then sank back down into her seat and watched him until he went out the door. She'd been through his tantrums before. Countless times. When this one subsided, maybe he'd listen to her. She knew she had to tell him the truth about Koo and herself. He'd be back. She'd wait. She looked at her watch. Almost one. She slid the pitcher toward her and refilled her glass.

3

ALDEN VINING woke up suddenly. He turned up the volume on the radio. The strains of Beethoven's Archduke Trio soothed his mind like a caress. Such beauty, he thought, such order. Once he had thought he could live his life with beauty and order. Once he'd thought that he had only to decide what was right and then pursue it, that he could craft a life like a symphony. That was before he began to understand what he was really like, what he was capable of. That was before Jacky.

Alden sat up. He grabbed for a tissue and sneezed, an explosion that roared in his ears and filled up his head. For a moment he savored the misery, then he blew his nose. He threw the tissue in the wastebasket by his bed and pulled another out of the box. Thank God I didn't have to go tonight, he thought. He pictured John Winston dressed in his tux, standing close to Jacky, his hand on her bare arm, touching her for all to see. He had a way of showing everybody that this beautiful woman was his possession, like his race horses, like his forty-foot yacht, like his goddamn Picassos.

Alden's eyes were red and teary. Thank God I got to miss this one, he thought again. He looked at the clock on his bedside table. One forty-seven. Long over by now. He felt another sneeze pushing against his eyes, his nose. He could see her with her head on John's shoulder, putting on an act. She was good at acting.

The phone rang. Alden was reaching for it when the sneeze erupted. He stopped with his arm in midair. Who could it be? he wondered. No one he wanted to hear from, that was for sure. His son in Taos calling with some new complaint, all boozed up, not even knowing what time it was? His daughter? Or something more troublesome, closer to home, something he wasn't even expecting? Sweating, his ears ringing, he reached for the phone. But whoever it was must've given up.

Maybe it was Jacky, he thought. Maybe she's missing me. If only he could be with her right now, although he didn't want to give her this lousy cold. He loved her. God, how he loved her. But did she really love him? He wanted her to tell him with her eyes, her hands, her body, how much she loved him. That it was all right, that everything would work out all right. No. Just that she loved him. That would be enough.

The phone rang again.

"Alden." It was Jacky. But something was wrong.

"What is it? Are you all right?"

"I have to talk to you. It's important."

"Where are you? I'll meet you." He was already swinging his legs off the bed.

"No. I'll come there. I have a quick stop to make first. Half an hour."

4

MATT TOOK DEEP BREATHS as he walked by the Bison Range toward the Elephant House. He always enjoyed his regular early morning walk around the zoo. Not only did it give him the opportunity to check the condition of the animals and the functioning of the zoo plant, but it allowed him time alone to think before his busy day began.

This morning the air was crisp. Fallen leaves cushioned the paths. The animals' breath made smoke puffs in the still air.

In the Elephant House, the odor of dung and hay, the rich musky smell of the animals rose with the heated air. Solomon lumbered toward him and stuck his trunk through the bars as usual. Matt held out a piece of apple from the bag he carried with him. The huge animal reached out with his trunk, gently took the fruit from Matt's hand, and curled it into his mouth.

"Something wrong, old feller?" Matt crooned as he petted the trunk, "or just age catching up with you?" He made a notation in the notebook he always carried on his morning tour. He'd spotted many an illness by observing changes in animal behavior or appearance. He believed that preventive medicine was one of the most important jobs in running a zoo.

Keepers were arriving for work and he chatted with them as they came on the job. Tom O'Rourke, the big cats head keeper, gave him a wave as he walked down the path toward the Big Cats House.

In front of the Primates Building rumpled paper napkins and plastic cups were scattered on the ground. Matt stood for a moment looking at the detritus of last night's Gala and he thought of Jacky, of the way her glowing face had opened to the crowd, the curve of her body as she bent toward the audience. Damn, damn, he muttered, kicking at the maple leaves that were as red as her dress. He closed his eyes, but that only made him see more vividly her white skin, the black skein of her hair.

Matt passed the tiger enclosure. Empty now. The tigers must be in their sleeping quarters in the Big Cats House. The smell of cat hung in the still air, acrid and strong. He headed up the hill toward the Bear Dens. This was his favorite part of the morning walk. From the path up the hill he could look down to the pond below, where ducks and geese hunted for food in the shallows. Overhead in a sky that was just beginning to take on the rosy hues of early morning, a wedge of geese was flying and honking. The sight stirred him. He sighed. You're longing for something that never existed, he told himself. She never really loved you and you idealized her into something she never was.

I'll be forty in a few weeks, he thought. Life begins at forty. Ha ha. He wondered if he would have married if he hadn't been stuck on Jacky or, rather, his vision of Jacky: daring, passionate, a cross between Tarzan's Jane and an Amazon warrior. The same shrink who told him he distanced himself from people by envisioning them as animals had told

19

him he'd never be able to love a real woman until he worked this idealized woman out of his head. That's when he'd decided therapy wasn't for him. He didn't want his dream destroyed, especially not by someone who charged seventy-five bucks an hour to do it.

Now at the top of the hill, Matt looked down through the bright fall foliage to the pond, rose-colored in reflected early morning light. He breathed deeply and smiled as the pieces of his world began to fall into a brighter pattern. Not yet forty and he was already the director of a zoo, his life-long dream realized. Because of Jacky. She had fought for him, pitted herself against her husband to give him this opportunity.

Walking through the pine grove toward the bear dens, the pattern shifted again. If it weren't for Jacky, he wouldn't be director. Several of the board members had wanted to bring in an outsider, someone who had proven himself. John Winston felt the post required someone with a strong business sense. Matt had little business experience. All his expertise was in animal management. He had to prove that he could do this job and do it well, this job requiring skill in so many areas. He quickened his step. He could do it. He'd learn what he didn't know. He'd already made a good start.

The first den was that of the Kodiaks. Tonto was standing and sharpening his claws at the huge pine that stood atop the ledge. Although the den was only fifty feet away, there seemed to be no barrier between the bear and Matt, because you didn't see the deep moat in front of the den until you were practically on top of it. Tamuka lay like an old brown fur coat on the ledge near Tonto, one paw draped over the edge in sleep. Stepping closer, Matt noticed a small patch of matted fur darkened with blood on Tamuka's side. An abscess? A wound given her by Tonto in a lovers' quarrel? He noted it in his book and moved on.

20

The corner den, the equivalent of the bridal suite in a fancy hotel, was the home of Anuk, the polar bear, and her two cubs. The male polar bear, Nanuk, had been moved out to another den last winter before Anuk gave birth because polar bear fathers have a tendency to harm their young. Poor Nanuk! To be denied the comforts of this luxury den with its shallow wading pool that flowed in a graceful waterfall to the swimming pool below, large enough for several bears to bathe and play in. Not a male's world. Not for Nanuk in any case. As Matt approached the den, he was struck by the unnatural silence of the place.

Something was wrong. Anuk was not outside, lying on the ledge nursing her cubs. She wasn't splashing in the pool with the cubs as she usually did at this hour. In fact, he couldn't see the white bear at all. But he did see something, something that made him run toward the den: a patch of red at the top of the den near the wading pool. He raced by the deep pool at the lower level and sprinted up the steep path. A ten-foot-high spiked iron fence separated him from the den's upper level. Out of breath, Matt stood at the top of the path looking down through the bars of the fence to the rocky wading pool below.

She lay on her back, her torso and legs angled across the wading pool, the bright red dress swirled around her knees. Her head hung over the rock ledge. At the base of her arched neck, the diamonds on her throat caught the sunlight through the shallow water. Her black hair poured down into the rush of the waterfall, like supple underwater weeds pulsing in the current. One of her arms dangled from the ledge. The other arm, stretched out beside her body, appeared to be torn away at the shoulder. Matt looked down at that shoulder, at blood, gristle, and bone. Then he vomited into the deep fall leaves beside the path.

5

LIEUTENANT IRVING COHEN of the Braeton police had seen plenty of disgusting sights in his thirty-year career, yet what always got to him the most was the waste of a life lost by accident or murder. Especially murder. Murder made him mad as hell. It was the arrogance of it, that someone could think he had the right to destroy another human being. It always made him sick. In this case, the victim had been young and beautiful. He looked up from where he was kneeling beside the body. The top of the iron fence was about ten feet above them. Had she climbed up on that fence of her own volition or had she been carried there, then dropped down? He bent over the woman's feet. Then he sat back on his haunches and looked more closely. He got up, walked around the body, and returned to her feet.

"Hughes, c'mere," he called.

The young detective propped his measuring tape against the fence and approached his boss.

Lieutenant Cohen pointed. "Take a look. Here." Then he turned to the paunchy older man who was packing his camera away into its case. "Hey, Clancy." He pointed again to the woman's feet. Hughes was looking at them with a puzzled expression on his face.

22

Obedient, Clancy got down into a deep knee bend and took a few more pictures, this time of the corpse's feet.

Cohen looked at Hughes's puzzled face and smiled. "Back to the office," he said. "We'll take statements there. You can tell me what you make of her shoes." They walked.

How could it have happened? Matt wondered as he sat waiting outside Lieutenant Cohen's office later that morning. She's been working with wild animals for years. She knew how to take care of herself. He sighed. She could've been drunk. She seemed to be drunk more and more often in the last few years. He tried to imagine her at the top of the fence. The swirl of her red dress, her bare shoulders and arms flashing white in moonlight as she danced on the narrow iron ledge. He could almost hear her laugh. See me. See me. I'm doing this crazy thing. She was—had been—a show-off, a narcissist. She would've been up there drunk on Scotch, drunk on her own courage. Proud of her guts, her power, her capacity to escape from ordinary life.

Suddenly it occurred to him that she wouldn't have been alone. No. She would've been out drinking with someone. Jacky was not a loner. He couldn't picture her climbing that fence alone unless . . . unless. No, she wouldn't commit suicide. He saw her again as she had looked last night at the Gala, arms outstretched, encompassing her world, all she had accomplished, bathed in the adulation of the crowd. Not someone about to give it all up. Yet it was true she was drinking more, and he knew she was unhappy with John. She'd told him a lot, over the years, about John's need for power, his lust for other women. Still, she'd never seemed suicidal, and recently he'd seen some secret happiness behind her eyes.

No. She wasn't suicidal and, if she were, she wouldn't

23

have set out to kill herself by jumping into Anuk's cage. He shivered. Not the death of choice, not by a long shot. And she wouldn't have gone there alone. But if she had been showing off for someone and had slipped and fallen into the cage, wouldn't her companion have tried to save her, have called for help?

Matt stood up and began to pace the little room. If it wasn't an accident and it wasn't suicide. . . . He sat down again, suddenly weak and exhausted. He smelled coffee and realized he was longing for a cup. He hadn't had breakfast. He'd been planning on coffee and a croissant later in his office, after his tour around the zoo.

But who could have had reason to murder Jacky? She wasn't the kind to make enemies. She liked people. Even when she fell out of love with someone, she did it graciously. He ought to know. They'd been friends for years. All the time that he was assistant curator in Worcester, Jacky had been planning to get him to Braeton. Not that Jacky didn't have faults, but she didn't make other people suffer for them.

The young police detective wearing the bright brown-checked jacket stood in the doorway of Lieutenant Cohen's office. "Mr. Yates. Please come in."

Matt stood up. He felt worn out by the horrors of the morning, and the day was only beginning.

Lieutenant Irving Cohen sat behind an old wooden desk, blowing his nose. He had the puffy red eyes of an allergic person or someone with a bad head cold. A large man with big features and thinning brown hair, he wore a dark gray suit. "Sit. Sit." He motioned to the chair across from his desk and Matt sank into it. "I'm sorry I had to get you over here. I'm sure you'll have a lot to do at the zoo today. But you can understand that I wanted to see you first, get this investigation under way."

Matt nodded. Cohen seemed polite, but Matt sensed a

24

toughness beneath his manner. He looked over at Officer Hughes, who sat near the window with a notepad on his knees.

"Hughes takes notes," Cohen explained following Matt's glance. "In this business, you don't want to forget a thing." He smiled.

Matt realized that he was offended by Cohen's casual manner, as if this had been a petty theft or even a robbery instead of Jacky's death. But then Cohen seemed to change, to become more sympathetic. "I'm sure you must still be in shock, discovering the body as you did. She was a friend?"

"A good friend."

Cohen looked closely at Matt. "You want coffee?"

Hughes was already getting up. "How do you want it?" he asked.

Matt's face brightened. "Milk?"

Hughes left the room and Cohen leaned back in his chair, blew his nose, then allowed the chair to spring back. "So, we'll make it short today. Anything else you want to tell me before I start my questioning?"

"Like what?"

Hughes was back with the coffee. Matt took the styrofoam cup in two hands and gulped. Hughes went around the desk and gave his boss a cup, black.

Cohen took a sip, made a face, and put the cup down on the desk. "How well did you know her?"

"I've known her for a long time, since college." Matt met Cohen's probing eye.

"And do you have any idea if there was anything bothering her, anything that might've been bad enough to make her dive into the bear's cage?"

Matt shook his head. "She wasn't like that. She loved life."

Cohen picked up the cup. "I'm wondering if you got any ideas about who might've found her a nuisance."

25

Matt was silent, then he shook his head.

Cohen concentrated on blowing his nose again. "Damn allergies. Every spring, every fall."

Matt looked out the window behind Cohen's head, eager to be somewhere else. He couldn't stop seeing that broken body, the brightness of the red chiffon gown, like a mockery of death, against the white, white limbs. Her head thrown back . . . "Her neck looked as if it was bent back in a funny way, like it was broken?"

Cohen shook his head. "Medical examiner thinks it wasn't actually broken." He waited, watching Matt. Then he said, "The heel of one of her shoes was missing."

Matt stared at him. It seemed so trivial. "What does that mean?"

"Well, we're wondering if the heel broke off when she fell—or jumped, but we couldn't find it."

"You looked for it?" Matt was surprised.

"We're combing the area. With the help of your bear keeper, we've examined the cage and the sleeping den. We drained the pool, and checked all the possible approaches to the cage. No sign of it. Not a sequin. What I want to know is, could the bear have, you know, swallowed it?"

"Swallowed the heel of her shoe?" Matt closed his eyes, seeing again what he didn't want to see: the torn arm and shoulder, muscle and guts exposed. He shook his head. "I don't know. From the look of it, I'd say Anuk attacked her when she jumped or fell in. But then after she killed her, Anuk was frightened off. The smell or whatever. They don't really like human smell. It upsets them. We know Anuk was very upset because she took her cubs into her sleeping quarters and didn't come out." Matt put his head in his hands. "Oh, it's horrible," he moaned. "What a way to die."

"The bear didn't kill her, if that makes you feel any better," Cohen said.

26

Matt raised his head from his hands.

"Dr. Edman, the medical examiner, thinks she died of the head wound, possibly received when she hit those rocks just under the fence."

"I don't get it. Why are you looking for the heel? What difference does it make if Anuk swallowed it or not?"

"It's a little hard to imagine her walking up the hill, climbing that fence, and balancing on the narrow ledge on the top without the heel of one of those sequined shoes."

"Why not?"

"You've obviously never tried walking in those stiletto high heels."

"You have?" Matt felt a flicker of amusement despite his despair, imagining the shaggy bearlike man balancing on a pair of high heeled shoes.

Cohen laughed appreciatively. "Let's say I've talked to experts about it. What I learned was, when a woman breaks the heel off one of those jobs, she can't walk in the shoes. What she does is, she takes off both shoes and walks in her stockinged feet until she gets the heel fixed or she gets into another pair of shoes. Walking in shoes with one heel on, one heel off is tough. Climbing up a fence with them on is damn near impossible.

"In fact, the right kind of shoes are very helpful in getting to the top of that fence. There's only one way up, by shinnying up the corner post. Officer Hughes, here, did it easily."

Hughes laughed and Cohen looked at him, then went on, "I had a little trouble myself." He looked down at his worn leather-soled shoes.

Matt followed his gaze to his shoes and then looked at his belly hanging out over the top of his trousers. His shirt was tight across the stomach. Matt could see his shoulder holster tucked neatly under his arm.

"Besides being twenty years my junior and a weight lifter,"

Cohen was saying, "Officer Hughes, you may notice, has rubber-soled shoes."

Hughes held up his big feet for inspection.

"Her shoes may have been more of a hindrance than a help in getting up the fence," Matt said, remembering the delicate sandals.

Cohen shrugged. "Possibly."

"You'd think she would've slipped them off, tried to climb without them," Matt continued his train of thought. "She was a good athlete and she was slim. . . ."

Cohen patted his belly affectionately. "Are you implying?"

Hughes laughed again, one bark, like the harbor seal.

Matt didn't laugh. "I guess, what you're telling me is that she wouldn't have walked up the steep slope to the high side of the bear pit in those shoes with a broken heel. The shoes must've been okay when she walked up the slope, shinnied up the pole. The heel must've broken off when she fell into the bear pit. But if the heel broke off then, when she fell, maybe even caused her fall into the bear pit, where is it?"

"The bear?" Cohen asked.

Matt frowned. "What did Mike say?"

"He also didn't think she'd ingest it, but he said he'd check the stool."

Matt nodded. "Still, when we do autopsies on the animals that die at the zoo, often we find in their stomachs everything from ten dollars in change to a kid's water pistol."

"So, if we don't find the heel of that shoe in the stool, it could be in the bear's stomach?"

"Could be, but I'd say that's unlikely. Anuk was afraid, that's why she attacked Jacky. Then she got as far away as she could, I'd guess, and stayed away."

"One other question before you go," Cohen said. "About the nighttime security at the zoo. How does that work exactly? Naturally, I'm interested in last night."

"Last night we posted a security guard at the gate to let people in and out until the Gala was over."

"And when was that?"

"Around midnight."

"Then what?"

"Then we went back to the usual nighttime system: every authorized person is issued a plastic card with his identification number that opens the gate. Time of entry and exit as well as card number are recorded electronically. But," Matt paused, remembering, "we didn't turn on the system immediately after the guard went off duty last night because there were still people in the zoo. I stayed until the last car left the lot and turned on the system when I left."

"What time was that?"

"I don't know exactly. A little after two thirty. The gate record will show the exact time."

"And where were you between midnight when the guard left and the time you turned on the system?"

Matt felt his skin prickling. "In my office, mostly."

Lieutenant Cohen stood up. "Thank you, Mr. Yates. We'll talk further. Please get me the gate record for last night as soon as possible."

Matt agreed and left.

6

"I TOLD YOU Mr. Yates is at police headquarters," the large woman said irritably. "I'll make another appointment for you next week." She slid her appointment book across the desk toward herself.

Lisa arched her back against the uncomfortable wooden bench. "I don't mind waiting. When he gets here, if he doesn't want to see me, he'll just say so."

The woman gave her a cold look. Lisa put her head down and pretended to read the copy of *Zoo Journal* on her lap. In a few moments she heard the sound of typing again. She looked at her watch. Twelve thirty. He was already over an hour late. How long would they keep him at police headquarters?

She had managed to get into the zoo just as they closed the gates. The place was crawling with police. She had seen the ambulance drive off. She had heard the news from the employees milling around the office until Matt's officious secretary shooed them away. Jacqueline Winston, the beautiful woman who had spoken with such passion at last night's Gala, was dead. Word around the zoo had it that she'd gotten drunk and fallen into the polar bear's den sometime in the early morning, that she'd been mauled to death by the she-bear.

Lisa tried to make herself unobtrusive in her corner of the bench. They'd have to drag her away to get her out of here now. She stole a look at the woman typing, a large pillowy woman with short-cropped curly gray hair and a round, but by no means pleasant, face. A bossy face, that was it, very bossy. Just the way she occupied her chair, Lisa could tell that she'd designated herself as Matt's protector.

She heard footsteps outside the office. The secretary did too. She jumped up and intercepted Matt at the door, then pointed to Lisa.

"Tell her to go. I can't get her to . . ." The rest was a whisper.

Matt looked her way. His face seemed white and drained.

"Matt," she said, starting to get up.

He was coming toward her, shaking his head slowly but kindly. "I'm sorry. I can't see you today. If you'll just . . ." he began. Then he stopped and put his arms out to her. "Lisa. Is it . . . ? I don't believe it. I don't." She fell into his arms, her face pushed up against his scratchy tweed shoulder. He hugged her hard, then held her away and smiled.

It was good to see his face change, she thought, good to see him come alive again.

"It's okay, Addie. Lisa's an old friend."

"The policemen at the dens asked that you get up there as soon as you got back from headquarters." Addie's face didn't look unpleasant to Lisa now, just worried.

"And I shall, I shall, after Lisa and I've had a reunion for about ten minutes. Now Addie, if you'll brew us a couple of cups of your terrific coffee and bring in some of those croissants you'll get a big raise."

The old biddy was actually smiling. Matt guided Lisa

31

toward his office, his arm around her. "You grew up without me," he scolded when she'd sat down beside his desk.

"Had to. You disappeared on me."

He shook his head slowly back and forth, still smiling. "Those were good years. Mom loved Anna so. How is she?"

"Good. How's Harry?"

Matt's face got so solemn that she knew before he said it. "Died. Two years ago."

Her hand searched for and found his on the desk. "I'm sorry."

"I know."

"They were two of a kind, our mothers," Lisa said. She was remembering Stella Yates's funeral. A cruelly beautiful morning in May. Birds singing their hearts out. Anna crying as she had never cried when her husband left her. After Stella's death, Lisa had seen Matt only once or twice. Harry Yates moved back to the Midwest. Matt was in college.

"You know, Mom was already sick when we moved to Brookline," Matt said.

"I didn't know that." She could almost see Stella's coppery curls framing a youthful face. Stella was always laughing. What Lisa remembered was Sundays driving in Harry's old car to Crane's Beach for picnics, Anna and Stella sitting cross-legged on the living room floor with the *Times* crossword puzzle, dinners at one or another of their apartments, and afterward, everyone doing dishes.

"Anna made her feel young again—for a while."

"And Stella saved Anna. Abe had just left us."

Matt nodded.

Her sigh seemed to fill her chest with its weight. She remembered that lonely time. The Yateses had come and filled their lives. Then they'd gone, leaving emptiness again. Just don't depend on anyone, the little voice in her brain piped up.

32

"I always meant to come back to see you. Life just galloped away, with me astride."

"You did write," she said. She knew how it was. She'd learned enough about life by now.

"Hey," Matt said, picking up her chin with his finger. "You remind me of Bagels."

Bagels. His basset hound. Gone now too, but she laughed.

Addie brought in coffee and a plate of croissants and watched lovingly as Matt bit into a croissant.

"This place is going to be a mess, Addie." Matt wiped his mouth with a paper napkin.

"Don't worry, Mr. Yates. I'll sort phone calls."

"I know. Addie's so good at that," he said to Lisa. "Addie, this is Lisa Davis, who was like my kid sister a long time ago. Addie Whitney, who runs this place."

Addie, all pussycat now, held Lisa's hand in a firm, fat paw.

"I have to get back up there," Matt said as they finished the coffee.

"Let me come with you?" Lisa asked. "I'm sure my editor will want me to do a piece on Mrs. Winston's death."

Matt shook his head. "I'm sorry. I promised the police I would allow no one at the scene. But why don't we have dinner tonight. I'll give you what you need for your piece and we can catch up on old times."

"I'd love it," she said, shrugging off the rejection. It had been worth a try, anyway. They agreed on the dining room at the Braeton Arms at seven.

Matt walked out of the building with her, and they hugged again before he headed up the hill.

Watching him go, Lisa felt a pang of disappointment. He wasn't what she'd expected. He was still sweet. But he wasn't a hero anymore to her. He'd lost it, that golden quality he used to have. Or maybe it was just that her expectations were

33

unrealistic, the vision of an adolescent. She walked back to her car, past a solitary policeman at the gate to the parking lot. She thought of Stella. Of Anna's bafflement when Absent Abe left. Of all the losses in her life.

———————⟫ ⊂———————

Lisa drove back to Main Street and parked in the *Times* parking lot. She entered at the back door and walked past the cluttered desks to her own cluttered desk. The room was empty except for the receptionist in a glass cubicle at the front. Everyone out to lunch.

She sat at her desk. What she'd really like to be doing was taking notes at the scene of Jacky Winston's death with Matt and the police. She didn't believe that the forceful woman she'd seen last night could be the victim of a drunken fall. She was sure there was more to it than that.

By the time the other reporters returned from lunch, she'd finished her article on the Gala and had a list of questions on her pad to ask Matt tonight. She'd also started work on a new idea—a feature series on the workings of the Braeton Zoo. She'd have to check it out with her editor Harry Trevera and then find out if Matt would agree to help her with it.

7

THE RESTAURANT at the Braeton Arms was called Mon Reve
and it looked like a dream. The ceiling was painted purple-
blue with clouds and stars and a silver moon. The booths
were covered with silvery pillows. Lisa felt as if she was
sinking into cobwebs as she pushed in next to Matt. A bottle
of white wine and two glasses were already on the table. A
waiter in a black tuxedo shook out her napkin and placed it
in her lap, filled her wine glass, then left them alone.

Lisa looked around. "Pricey," she whispered.

Matt waved it away. "I make a big salary and I've got no
one to spend it on."

"There's you," she pointed out.

He smiled. "What about you?"

"Me?"

"You got someone to spend your big salary on?"

Lisa laughed, thinking of her $17,500 per annum. "Anna.
But it's more the other way around. She's the big spender.
I'm supposed to be saving for my hope chest."

"Hope chest. Hmm." He looked at her carefully.

"Anna can't wait to see you," Lisa said. "Can you come
to dinner on Sunday?"

"Gladly. I meant to call her before now."

"Don't worry, she understands. Anna always understands. She understands me so well she knows what I'm thinking before I know it myself." Lisa sipped her wine. "Except . . ." The wine made her feel afloat in this dreamy room.

"Except?"

"The hope chest."

"Oh, I see. Have you ever . . . ?"

"Married? You can say it. Nope. I've tried. Never worked. I mean, I've tried to find someone to marry. See?"

"I see. Me too."

"I always thought . . ." she began, then stopped.

"What?"

"Well, growing up, I thought you were just about perfect. I don't understand why you haven't been gobbled up."

"Perfect? Me? Anyway, it's not so easy, to find the right person who also believes you're the right person."

Lisa put down her glass. "Anna doesn't believe that. She thinks it's only my orneriness that has kept me from it. I can't wait for her to see you. She always thought you did everything right. You could be a big help. We could even marry each other."

"Hey, I'm too old for you," He refilled her glass.

"I'm almost thirty-two." She paused. "And I'm not sure I like it. I may have to pretend to be twenty-nine again."

"You don't impress me as the kind of woman to be obsessed with popular standards of youth."

She sat back. "I like that. I like you. It's all coming back. Wait'll Anna gets her claws into you. Eligible young man. Jewish even." Lisa giggled.

"I remember that giggle."

Lisa sipped her wine. It was fruity yet tart. She looked at the label. Vouvray.

"Like it?" he asked.

"Mmm."

"The last time I saw you, you were a kid. After Stella died."

"It was when you came home to help your dad pack up. I was fifteen."

He nodded. "Long time ago." He sat sadly, twirling his glass by the stem. "You were writing poetry. You wrote a poem about Mom. You gave it to me and I've kept it."

She nodded, remembering. The poem had been about their mothers shopping together for vegetables at the peddlers' carts in the Faneuil Hall marketplace. Long before it became fashionable. "I don't write poetry much anymore since writing has become my profession."

"What did you do before the *Times?*"

"I did PR for a high-tech company for a while. Then I got an M.A. in Journalism at Addison. My moves have been somewhat lateral because I had trouble figuring out what I wanted to do. Then I had trouble figuring out how to do it."

"So now you're doing what you want?"

"Sort of. I want the exciting stuff. I'd like to specialize in crime reporting."

"Isn't that a little dangerous for a woman?"

She looked at him sharply. Condescending? No. Not Matt.

"Crime is dangerous, not crime reporting," she said. "Anyway, I can take care of myself."

"I didn't mean to insult you." He was laughing. She could tell he liked her toughness. And all of a sudden she remembered how he'd treated her like an equal and encouraged her desire for independence when she was a girl.

Now seemed like a good time to present her idea. "I'd like to do a feature series on the zoo. My editor thinks it's a great idea. We could have a little about the zoo's history, goals. I could interview keepers and department heads, give an inside view of the zoo and maybe end up with an overall view—you could write that if you wanted."

"I don't see why not. Sounds like good PR, and, God knows, we could use some now. Would you mind if I okay your copy?"

"That's all right."

"And are you still working on the article about Jacky's death?"

"I am. My editor wants it. I knew he would. I was hoping you could fill me in."

He sighed. "In a bit. I need to unwind a little."

"Sure." They sipped wine silently. Then Lisa said, "You know, when I was assigned to the Braeton Zoo Gala story, I thought it would be routine. Then I read up on it and discovered you'd been the director since last spring. I was surprised."

He looked down. "I've thought of calling ever since I came back to town. I even looked up Anna's number and saw it hadn't changed. I wanted to call, but I didn't know if I could take it, going back to St. Paul Street, seeing Anna again."

"I can understand that."

"But I want to see her. I would've called sooner or later."

The waiter stood over them. They studied the silver menus. "The crab here is very good," Matt told her.

"I'll try it."

"Make that two," Matt said to the waiter.

Music started up. *The Four Seasons*. Lisa felt warmed by the wine and the music. She bit into hot French bread with melting butter. "You'll tell me all about the investigation?" she asked again.

"Jacky Winston was an old friend of mine. I've known her since college."

Matt said it simply, but Lisa knew there was more. She'd seen the way he'd looked at her. "It must be terrible for you."

"It is. About Jacky. And also because the zoo is in an uproar and likely to remain so for quite a while."

"Do you think it could've been an accident?"

"Probably not. The police are looking into it."

Lisa had heard people at the zoo say Jacky might've gotten drunk and fallen in. "Why don't they think it was an accident?"

Mat rubbed a hand across his forehead. "I don't think I can talk about it yet. Wait 'til I hear more. I'll see the police tomorrow and I'll pass on anything I can to you."

Lisa hoped he wasn't giving her a runaround. But she could see he was in pain.

"In fact," he said, "why don't you come by tomorrow? I'll introduce you to some people who can help you with your feature stories."

Lisa brightened. "When?"

"I've a meeting with the architects that'll probably last until ten thirty or so. Can you make it eleven?"

"I'll be there."

They talked about everything but Jacky Winston, through the soft-shelled crab and the salad, through more wine and coffee. Lisa felt relaxed. Matt brought her back through the years to the time when the Yateses had been such good friends. Cheerful Stella, accommodating Harry, and Matt, who had been gentle and kind to her when she was a lonely little girl after Abe left, just walked out on them one day when she was five.

She told him how she'd come to call her mother Anxious Anna over the years, how as Anna got stronger herself, she seemed to focus all her anxieties on her. "She claims she doesn't understand why I want to live in my own apartment," Lisa said, laughing. She told him about her mother's rise to the position of toy buyer at Cummings'. "And she's good, really good at it. She's as enthusiastic about the toys as a child."

"Why is she so anxious about you?" he asked.

The waiter refilled their coffee cups.

"Truly she won't be satisfied until I'm married. You'd think, after what she went through, she wouldn't be so eager to marry me off. But I guess she feels if I do it and do it right, it'll make up for everything."

Matt looked at her over his coffee cup and smiled. "So, why don't you oblige the poor lady, give her some peace?"

Lisa shrugged. "Marriage might be okay, but so far I've had terrible luck with men." She went on to tell him about the several men who had been important to her.

It wasn't until after they'd said goodnight and she was driving home to Cambridge in the rain that she realized how little Matt had said about his personal life.

8

IT WAS STILL DARK at six Tuesday morning when Koo approached the front gate of the zoo. There was a light on in the gatehouse and, as he walked toward it, he could see a man dressed in blue sitting at the desk reading a newspaper.

Damn, Koo thought. Just what I need. Cops everywhere. But of course he had known that they would be.

Usually when he arrived early, he would insert his plastic ID card in the slot that released the turnstyle and recorded the time. Most mornings he was the first employee at the zoo and he liked it that way. He'd arranged with his boss Tom O'Rourke that he could come as early as he wanted to do his chores. Sometimes he would stay until zoo closing. Other times he'd leave in the middle of the afternoon. The zoo was more of a home to him than the dingy little room on Ward Street. He was at his happiest here among the exotic animals who knew and respected him. With people, on the other hand, he always felt as if he was the one who belonged to some rare and exotic species.

Now he impatiently stamped his booted feet while the policeman inspected his card and wrote down everything on it. Because the policeman's notebook was empty except for the information that he was now copying into it, Koo knew that no one had gotten here before him this morning, and he was glad. He looked forward to the time alone with his cats before Tom arrived.

Koo looked up at the sky. He liked the transparent pre-dawn gray, as if the black of night was being drained out of the sky before the lavish early dawn colors were poured in.

Aware of the policeman studying his profile in the light from the gatehouse, he tossed his head, flipping back the straight blond hair that fell over his forehead. It was a gesture he had practiced in his early teens because he liked the way it made him feel, but by now it was natural to him. He slowly turned his head. His large eyes, which were either slate gray or ice blue depending on what he was wearing, settled on those of the policeman and watched steadily.

The policeman shifted in his seat, embarrassed. Koo allowed the slow smile for which he was famous to spread from his lips up to his eyes. The policeman cleared his throat and thrust the card at Koo. He was young and unattractive with frizzy black hair, a long nose, and acned skin. Not someone Koo would ever touch or be touched by.

Koo smiled as he took back the card. He pushed through the turnstyle and headed toward the Big Cats House. He had unsettled the ugly young man in some way, made him think.

The tigers had been fed last night and they were sleeping like a couple of kitty cats outdoors near the door to their sleeping quarters. They'd probably gone inside during the rain and moved back out when it stopped. Another week or two and the cold would bring them indoors to sleep every night.

In the Big Cats House Koo put on a coverall over his shirt and jeans and pulled on high rubber boots over his boots. He pressed the switch on the wall next to the cage that closed the iron door between the cage and the indoor sleeping quar-

42

ters. Zoo rules were strict on the subject of cage security, and Koo had seen enough, anyway, to be very cautious. Tom O'Rourke, himself, had once been attacked and severely mauled by a half-grown tiger.

Koo hosed down the cage. Then he got the mop and bucket from the service shed behind the building. He mopped the cage with a disinfectant solution and then hosed it off again, making sure the walls and the feeding and water trays were clean. When he was satisfied, he filled the water tray with fresh water from the hose and left the cage. Outside, he locked the door and pressed the switch again, opening the door between the cage and the sleeping area so that the animals were free to go in and out at will.

Later, as Koo was sweeping the walk in front of the Big Cats House, a police car drove up the road toward the dens. He wasn't sure of the time. He never wore a watch. A watch was a hazard when working close to the big cats because they were attracted to anything shiny. He guessed that it was a little before eight. Tom hadn't arrived for work yet. He looked up as the car passed. The handsome young policeman was driving, with the fat old lieutenant, who was conducting the investigation, sitting next to him. Koo hurried to the back of the building. He moved silently through the trees and crouched behind a bush. From there he could see through the woods to the bear dens.

Three men were bending over in front of Anuk's den, the two he had seen drive up a few moments before and a young uniformed officer he didn't recognize. As he watched, the fat lieutenant straightened up, rubbing his back. Koo could hear his voice clearly. "Then why didn't those jerks find it yesterday?"

The uniformed man muttered something.

The fat man said, "You what?" and flung his arms up and out.

"I'm sorry, Lieutenant," the man in uniform said. Koo could see he was very young and very nervous.

"Jesus," the lieutenant shouted, looking up at the sky as if expecting an answer. "What they're giving us these days." Then he turned back to the young officer. "One simple job we give you. To stay awake. So you fall asleep."

The young man looked down. "I know. I'm sorry, sir."

"And how long was this siesta of yours?" the lieutenant barked at him.

"Only a matter of minutes."

The lieutenant shook his head wearily and looked at the man who had been driving the car. "Okay, Hughes, get to work on the so-called evidence. We'll do the best we can.

"You can go back to your post, go back to sleep," he shouted at the one in blue.

"Yes, sir." He shuffled off, out of view, and Koo slipped out of the woods and back to his chores.

9

As soon as Matt walked into the office Addie said, "You are not going to like this one."

What now? Matt thought. What else could possibly happen?

"Mr. Winston's secretary called. He wants you immediately for a meeting in his downtown office."

"What!" Matt cast a hopeless glance toward the door to his own office where he pictured the mounds of papers rising unchecked like bread dough in a warm room. "What's he doing there? He's supposed to be in mourning. Jacky's been dead one day and he's calling a goddamned meeting . . ." He stopped short.

Addie nodded. "That's what I thought, too. Maybe something's wrong."

Matt was already at the door. He waved toward his office. "Cancel the meeting with the architects. Clear whatever you can."

Addie was only too glad, he thought, as he hurried back to his car. She'd take over the whole job if he let her. The good part was she really saved him a lot of routine paperwork. The bad part was he still had so much to learn that he felt he needed to see everything in order to know exactly what was going on in every area of the zoo. He drove across town to Winston's office.

Winston's long-necked secretary, balanced on high heels like a wading bird on long legs, showed him into the conference room.

John Winston sat at the head of the table. On one side of him was Alden Vining, the treasurer of the Braeton Zoological Society, and on his other side sat George Finn, Matt's head animal nutritionist, who was in charge of all food purchases for the zoo. Then there was Susan Neiman, the head of accounting, and Sidney Krantz, the city auditor who was examining the zoo's financial condition before the city of Braeton would grant the increase in revenue the zoo had requested.

"What's going on?" Matt asked Winston.

Winston's face was flushed in splotches. He pushed his glasses up on top of his bald head. "Believe me, Matt," he began heavily, "this is the last place in the world I want to be today. I should be home with my family. Johnny's taking Jacky's death very hard. He's under a doctor's care. Sedated. Jacky's family is staying at the house. . . ." He paused, stared into space.

Everyone was silent, respectful, waiting for him to go on. He sat for a few moments toying with the ballpoint pen in his hands. His bald skull shone in the overhead light like an ocean-smooth piece of pink quartz. His eyes were heavy-lidded, as if he hadn't slept at all. Probably didn't, Matt thought.

"Sit down." Winston pointed to a chair next to Krantz.

The quick look of anger and reproach Winston gave him as he slid into the indicated seat brought Matt's attention back to himself. What was this all about, and what did it have to do with him?

46

Winston pushed some papers toward him. "Take a look at these."

They were requisition forms. Matt flipped through them. There were five. He noticed that his signature was on the bottom of each. He looked through them again and saw that all the requisitions were made out to the same company— A.C.E. Grain—that the ordering department was nutrition, and that George Finn's signature authorized each. The writing on the forms had been done through a carbon sheet, which meant that they were copies of the originals. There seemed to be one requisition per month sometime around the third week of each month. The first one was dated May seventeenth, the last September twenty-second. They were for amounts of somewhere between ten and fifteen thousand dollars.

Matt looked up from the papers, directly at John Winston. "I don't understand. What's wrong?"

Winston nodded toward Krantz. "Please, Mr. Krantz."

Krantz put the fingers of his small hands together. They were impeccably groomed. Wild gray hair surrounded his head like a fur hat, silver in the light. He began in a neutral voice, "As you know, I've been working on the Braeton Zoo books for the past two weeks."

Matt nodded. Of course he knew. He'd been the one to provide many of the necessary documents. He and Alden Vining and Susan Neiman and, of course, Addie, who had dug out the records from her files.

"In the course of our examination," Krantz continued, "we have come upon certain irregularities."

Matt felt a hot surge of blood to his cheeks. He tried to calm himself. "What do you mean?" he asked in what he hoped was an even voice. "And why haven't I been the first one contacted?" He felt like one of those characters in a Kafka

47

story, dragged before a tribunal and accused of some crime without even knowing what the crime was. He turned toward George Finn, his food expert, who seemed to be sitting in judgment against him. "What are you doing here, George?"

Before George could answer, Winston said in a weary voice, "Calm down, Matt. Nobody's accusing you of anything. Going over the books, Mr. Krantz noticed that food costs have tripled in the last several months compared with the same period of last year. Now, even allowing for a rise in cost due to inflation and for additional animals acquired since last year, there is still more than a sixty percent increase over costs for the same period last year. Were you aware of that?"

"No." Matt glanced again at George, who was looking down at the table. "But why wasn't I notified immediately? Why am I called in this way after you've clearly discussed the discrepancy with everyone else?" He felt powerless to control his rising voice.

"There was no intent to accuse you of anything," Winston said evenly. "The reason you weren't consulted sooner was only because we—Mr. Krantz and I—began with those who made the actual food decisions, who dealt with the providers. We thought the matter could be handled at that level. We discovered it couldn't."

Matt tried to push down his anger, but he knew that Winston's attitude toward him was laced with a hostility that Winston himself probably didn't even recognize for what it was. Privately, Matt had always believed that Winston disliked him because of his closeness to Jacky.

"What, exactly, is the matter with these?" Matt asked, waving the requisitions.

"What's wrong," Winston said, clearly anxious himself, "is that there is no A.C.E. Grain and Feed Company."

Matt turned to George Finn, who was looking down at

48

his hands, his usually genial round face red with embarrassment.

"Your signature, George," Matt said softly, pointing to the rather blurred signature on the copy in his hand.

George was shaking his head, his face even redder.

Mr. Krantz spoke up in a voice that was still neutral, "Mr. Finn claims this is not his signature."

Matt held the requisition closer. The ink of the copy was a uniform black. The signature beside the printed words "authorized by" suddenly looked as amorphous as an ink blot.

"The original . . ." Matt said, already beginning to understand.

John Winston was shaking his head. "No original in the treasurer's file. And only two copies. These, from your file, and the ones in the accounting department file, stamped paid."

Matt looked to Alden Vining, who had been very quiet throughout the discussion.

Alden shook his head, then looked away, somewhere over Matt's head.

Matt stared at the sheets in his hand. The system was simple. Each requisition had an original and three copies. The requesting department filled out the form and sent it to the director for approval. Matt signed if he approved the expenditure. Addie kept a copy for her files and brought the original and the two remaining copies to the treasurer's office. The treasurer kept the original. One copy was sent to accounting and one to the department making the request. Thus, both Matt and Alden Vining had a record of all expenditures. The department making the request had the signed requisition, which authorized it to make the order. And the accounting department had a record of the authorized requisition so that when the bill from the provider came, it could be paid.

All neat and tidy, with built-in checks and balances. Except —there was no original of the requisitions in question, there was no A.C.E. Grain and Feed Company, and George Finn had not signed the requisitions.

Matt flipped through the papers again. May seventeenth. Only a month after he'd taken over the job. He let out a short bark of laughter.

Everyone looked at him, startled.

"I was just thinking," he said, "I'd have to be some kind of stupid embezzler to start siphoning off funds right after I took over as director."

From the embarrassed expressions of all seated around the table, Matt guessed he had hit on what each of them was thinking at this moment.

Matt slid the requisitions back across the table to Winston. "I take it you've checked the copies in accounting's files along with the copy of the bill."

Krantz handed him a slip of paper. "This is the last bill received." A.C.E. Grain and Feed Company, P.O. Box 137, Newton Center, Mass. 02159 was imprinted across the top of a standard bill form. Under the heading the date had been typed. Matt noticed that it was September thirtieth. And under the date was typed, "Mixtures of oat and rye grain, plus other feed supplied in September, $11,962." Across the bottom of the bill was the accounting department's red "paid" stamp and the date.

Matt sighed and handed the bill back to Krantz. "I don't suppose you thought to do anything about fingerprinting," he suggested.

Krantz scratched his bushy gray head. "It never occurred to me. We could try now."

Matt nodded. "Might as well. If you haven't called in the police yet, you'd better." He turned back to Winston, "When did this well-hidden investigation begin?"

"Mr. Krantz came to me about ten days ago with his suspicions about the increase in food costs."

"Hmm. That would be around the second week in October. Interesting that there's been no October requisition. When did the board find out about the audit?"

"First week in October."

"So it seems that our embezzler also knew about the audit and stopped his operation."

Winston didn't respond to Matt's theorizing. Instead, he asked, "You didn't think the amounts of these bills excessive?"

"I didn't really question them. I had so many other demands on my attention, I guess I just relied on George's judgment—or what I thought was his signature." Matt stopped talking as he realized that what he'd said was damaging to him.

Winston also was silent, letting Matt's admission hang in the air for all to hear.

Matt remembered well that Winston had disapproved of his appointment because of his inexperience. Now Winston's silence seemed to say, I was right. Even if not actually a thief, Matt Yates is not competent as zoo director, just as I said.

George Finn broke the silence. "Of course, Matt wouldn't have known those kinds of details. He saw my signature on the requisition, so he signed it."

Matt smiled at George, simian with his worried, close-together eyes and long muscular arms. "Thanks, George," he said. Then he looked back at Winston. "I'm afraid that's all I know. You ought to talk to Addie. She's been here a long time. Maybe she has some ideas about this."

"We intend to," Winston said. "but we didn't want to speak to her without speaking to you first."

Matt looked around at his employees whom Winston had spoken to first. Then he quickly left the room.

51

10

As he drove back to the zoo, Matt mentally added up the sums that had been paid out to A.C.E. Grain and Feed Company during the five months that the bogus requisitions had passed his desk. At ten to twelve thousand a month, the total came to well over $50,000, a substantial amount, certainly.

Matt parked in his space and reentered his office. He explained the situation to Addie and watched her face change. First amazement, then worry.

"Do you remember those A.C.E. requisitions?" he asked.

"Yes. They were among the papers I gave to Mr. Krantz. Now I'd like to see them again."

"You'll see them. Winston's going to talk to you." He leaned over her desk and asked gently, "Tell me what you do with a requisition from the moment it arrives on your desk."

"Well, first I bring it in to you. When you've signed it, you put it here in my work box." She pointed to a half-filled wire basket. "I check the forms to make sure your signature went through the carbons and I detach our copy and file it. Then I take the original and the other two copies, still attached with the carbons in between, to Mr. Vining's office."

"When you take the forms to Vining's office, where do you put them?"

"Usually I give them to Lorna Quentin. But if she's not in the office I put it into her work basket."

"But usually she's there?"

Addie nodded. "There've only been a few times when I've left the forms in her basket."

"And what does Lorna do with them?"

Addie shrugged. "Well, I never asked her, but she has to show each requisition to Mr. Vining for his approval. That's the whole point, isn't it? For the treasurer to keep track of zoo expenditures, without having to ask the director about it, I mean?"

"Yes," Matt agreed. "I guess what I'm getting at is, could our thief steal a requisition and destroy the original and one of the copies before Mr. Vining got a look at it? This happened five times, don't forget. Could the thief have gotten to them in Lorna's basket five times and destroyed all but the copy that went to accounting?"

Addie looked thoughtful. "It would be improbable. But of course Mr. Vining is only here two or three times a week. So I guess once Lorna puts the requisition on his desk, it could sit there for a long time before he had a chance to look at it—days even."

"That's true."

"Another thing," Matt said. "Would Lorna read the requisition? Before she brought it in to Alden?"

"What do you mean?"

"I mean, would she notice that the requisition was made out to A.C.E.? And would she notice whether or not the requisition came back from Mr. Vining to be filed?"

53

"I don't know." Addie looked worried.

Matt was already moving toward the door. "I'll just talk to her myself. Back soon."

"Matt," Addie called as he opened the door.

He turned back.

"Nothing," Addie said. "It'll wait."

Walking down the hall toward the treasurer's office, Matt felt a blast of anger that made his head pound. He didn't like the way they'd treated him. Even Alden, whom he'd considered a friend of sorts, hadn't been any better than the rest. He hoped Alden wasn't in his office now. He wanted to talk to his secretary undisturbed.

Lorna Quentin was hard at work at her desk, nails clicking on keys like tap dancers as she put a column of figures into her computer. He waited until she paused, fingers arched over the keys, and cleared his throat.

Lorna looked up. "Mr. Yates," she said, surprised, owlish in large round glasses, a white scarf, like feathers, at her neck.

"Sorry to disturb you, but I wanted to ask you a few questions."

"Yes?" Alarm ruffled Lorna's features.

"I'm sure you've heard there's a little problem about some missing requisitions that should've been in the treasurer's files."

She nodded. "You mean the A.C.E. requisitions?"

"That's right. Do you remember them?"

"No," she said, panic in her voice. "Mr. Vining asked me about them. As I told him, I don't keep track of the requisitions that come in from your office. That's Mr. Vining's job. I just give them to him along with all the other documents that need his attention."

"But you do file the forms after he's looked at them?"

54

"Yes."

"And wouldn't you remember the ones you had filed?"

"Not necessarily." Her voice had risen, sharp and birdlike. "Because I file so many, you see. Look, I'll show you." She pulled open a drawer in the bank of files behind her desk. There were sheafs of folders filed in back of a label that said FEED. Each folder had the name of a company. "Able Farms" was the first, the name typed on a white label. Lorna held the folder open. Inside were requisitions arranged chronologically. "Greens," she pointed out. The next folder was "Appleton Orchards." Lorna held open the space between Able Farms and Appleton Orchards. "If there were an A.C.E. Grain Company, this is where it would be. There isn't. So I didn't make one."

Matt looked carefully at her. He felt certain that if he had typed a label that read A.C.E. Grain Company and attached it to a folder, and then over a period of five months filed five separate requisitions in that file, he would remember doing so. "Are you saying, then, that it is possible that you did make a folder for A.C.E. Grain when the first requisition came in last May, and then filed that requisition and the four that came in the following months, and that you might have forgotten doing so?"

She listened, her head cocked to one side, her eyes blinking rapidly. "No," she said firmly. "It would be there if I had."

Matt watched her as she pulled a paper clip apart. He thought about rephrasing his question, then decided against it. "Okay, thanks, Ms. Quentin," he said and left the office, puzzled.

Addie was waiting for him nervously. "No good, huh?" she asked when she caught his expression.

"You didn't tell me that she doesn't remember things."

"Just a little hardening of the arteries."

"You serious?"

"All too. Poor Lorna. Her memory's going. She's panicky about it."

Matt shook his head. "How old is she?"

"Early sixties."

"Will it get worse?"

"No one knows. It may, or it may stay the same."

"How can she work that way?"

"Well, she tries to compensate for it. She writes lists and, basically, her tasks are simple."

Matt started for his office.

"Matt?"

He turned.

Addie was sniffing in, something she did when she was tense. "You were . . . you were tactful about it, weren't you? All this questioning is going to be hard on her."

"For God's sake, Addie, I didn't even know what was the matter with her." Then he had a thought. "Does Mr. Vining know about this?"

"Yes. And he's been wonderful. She thinks he's God."

In his office Matt sat and looked out the window at the tiger enclosure. Raji and Rani were lying in the sun, their fur glowing. Matt glanced at the piles of papers on his desk, then back out the window, but the view that usually gave him so much pleasure held no enjoyment for him today.

Someone had been stealing zoo funds and probably would have continued to steal if it hadn't been for the audit. Someone had placed the requisition form with its three copies in Addie's workbox not just once, but five times. But when? What time of day? Had she ever seen the person who did it?

He got up and went into the outer office. Addie handed him some letters. "If you sign these now, I'll drop them in the mail on my way to lunch."

The letters related to a meeting of zoo directors in January at which he would be on a panel. He signed them. "Would you remember when you found those requisitions in your box?"

"I've been thinking about nothing else ever since you told me about the theft, and I know that I never saw any of them come in. Usually Terry Simone from nutrition brings the nutrition requisitions. I'm pretty sure that those A.C.E. requisitions were always in my box when I came in in the morning. I did notice that A.C.E. was a new company. But George has always switched around. He's always made deals."

"Did you notice anything unusual about the amounts?"

"I'm sorry. Maybe I should have, but I didn't. I was aware that there were still requisitions for feed from National Grain, but I just assumed that George was using both suppliers." Addie looked pained.

"It's all right," Matt assured her. "Not your fault." He started back into his office, then he remembered Lisa. He checked his watch. Almost eleven. "I'm expecting Lisa at eleven," he said. "Would you please send her in."

Back in his office, he stood at the window watching the two gold and black cats asleep in the sun. He put his hand to his forehead. His head was pounding. He kept seeing Addie's worried face. How can I distrust her? he asked himself. She's done everything in her power to make my taking over the zoo as smooth as possible. She's a decent person. He turned abruptly from the window. Of course it wasn't Addie.

He looked at the piles of papers on his desk. How much simpler life had been when he started out. He'd been an animal attendant then. He'd worked directly with the animals. He'd fed them, cleaned their cages. He'd gotten to know just about every kind of exotic animal in captivity. He understood animals, for God's sake. Unlike humans, they were understandable. But of course he'd known he couldn't be a keeper all his life.

He sat down. Whoever planned the theft had done a thorough job of it. It was someone who'd taken advantage of his being new to the job and inexperienced in the financial aspects. It had never occurred to him to check the expenditures against last year's even though he had those figures in his files. He had examined the requisitions to determine what each department needed. Sometimes he had talked with a department head when he questioned the validity of an order, but usually the orders had seemed reasonable. In the case of the nutrition department, he had relied completely on George Finn's judgment. He'd known George for years, had worked with him at the Worcester Zoo at one time.

He tried to think out the steps that the thief must have taken. First of all, he got possession of a requisition form. That was easy enough to do; every department had a supply of them. Then he invented a fictitious feed provider and typed in the form, giving amount of feed and cost. Then he signed George Finn's name in a fair enough imitation of George's signature so that no one would question it. He managed to deliver the requisition to Addie's box without being seen doing so. And finally, he removed the requisition that Addie put in Lorna Quentin's work box before she brought it in to Alden, who claimed he had never seen any of the requisitions. And he delivered the copy to the accounting department, which paid each bill when it came in and stamped their copy paid. What's more, he did it on five separate occasions.

Who could the thief be? Clearly someone who knows the routines of the zoo thoroughly. Someone who has access to department offices, and who wouldn't be noticed if he walked into the treasurer's office and into Matt's office. Or someone who had a key to either office. Alden himself fit the description perfectly. But that was absurd. Fifty or sixty thousand would be like petty cash to Alden, who ran an immensely successful software company and performed the treasurer's job only as a public service.

Matt stood up, suddenly desperate for fresh air.

"I'll wait for Lisa outside, then do my rounds," he told Addie. "I'll bring my beeper in case you need me for anything."

Addie nodded sympathetically.

11

OUTSIDE the air was fresh and crisp, cleansed by the rains of last night. It had been only a day since he'd found Jacky's body. It seemed like a month. Matt sat on the concrete step in front of the building, his chin in his hand. He saw Lisa enter the zoo through the turnstyle. She was wearing a brown tweed suit and her heels clicked on the asphalt path. When she saw him, she quickened her pace.

"What's wrong?" She sat next to him on the step.

"Trouble. Plenty of it." He looked into her eyes. They were a deep brown. "I have to know that you'll keep this strictly to yourself."

"I promise."

"If you think that, as a reporter, you can't keep it secret, you've got to be honest with me."

Lisa watched his profile—the narrow, bony face, the long thin nose, his mouth set with tension. "I want to help you, Matt. That's what's most important to me. You know that."

He nodded. "I've been thinking about getting a lawyer, and I may yet. But what I need now is to sort out what's been happening." Then he told her about the theft.

When he'd finished, she asked, "And you think the police suspect you?"

"I can see where they might."

"Other people had access to those requisitions."

"They know that."

"Who could have done it?"

Matt shrugged. He felt helpless, overwhelmed by bad luck.

Lisa looked at him with concern. He's so vulnerable, she thought, a lonely man sunk into himself. "You're checking it out?"

"Sure. We're all working on it." He didn't sound optimistic.

They got up and walked toward the Elephant House. The elephants were outside in the yard. Hugo Tollich, the head keeper, was examining the jaw of the largest of the elephants, his hand resting on the animal's cheek. A group of schoolchildren, standing by the fence, were watching the elephant's every move. An old man was watching too, sitting on a bench and eating peanuts from a bag.

When Hugo saw Matt arrive with Lisa, he walked over to the wall in front of the moat, the elephant following slowly. "Bad business," Hugo said, shaking his head. He was, of course, referring to Jacky's death, Matt knew. The news of the theft hadn't spread through the zoo yet.

Matt nodded. He didn't want to talk about any of it, but he didn't want to be rude. "I'd like you to meet Lisa Davis, an old friend. She's working on a feature series about the zoo. I'd appreciate it if you would talk with her."

"Pleased to meet you," Hugo said. "I could talk to you tomorrow."

"Fine. Any time you say."

"Anytime tomorrow morning. Earlier is better."

Solomon reached his trunk across the moat and Matt petted

it and held a piece of apple out to him, but Solomon wasn't interested. A bad sign, Matt thought.

"I'm watching the jaw," Hugo said. "Vet'll be in this afternoon."

Matt looked at the swelling on Solomon's jaw and nodded.

"What's the matter with him?" Lisa asked.

"An infected molar," Matt explained.

"Police everywhere," Hugo said. "For how long?"

"Not much longer. I hope," Matt replied as he started to walk on.

Matt and Lisa climbed the hill and looked down at the pond, dazzling now in late morning sunlight. Some gulls flashing silver wings were descending on the surface.

"They always know how to find an easy meal," Matt said.

At the top of the hill Matt paused at the path that led to the Bear Dens. He could see a corner of the first den and hear voices. He thought he heard Lieutenant Cohen's voice and realized that the quality that made it distinctive was a dark humor, a kind of irony, that was always present.

"What are the police doing here today?" Lisa asked.

"Still checking the area around the bear den." Matt didn't mention Jacky's heel. Cohen had told him not to.

They turned left toward the Big Cats House. The sounds from the Bear Dens grew louder as the path curved in that direction. The dens were directly behind the Big Cats House on the other side of the pine grove. They could hear the crackle of a walkie-talkie through the trees.

Inside the Big Cats House, the tiled lobby was freshly washed. The cages, too, were clean. The place smelled of disinfectant. In the lion's cage, Koo, the assistant keeper, was pouring water into the metal drinking pan. A few visitors were looking for the cats, but most of the cats were outside this morning.

As they walked into the lobby, Koo looked up and tossed

his head, flicking the golden hair out of his eyes. "Good morning." He waited to see if Matt wanted anything of him.

"How're Diego and Rosa?" Matt asked, glancing at the jaguars' cage.

"Ate well. Normal stools."

Matt smiled at him to cover the uneasiness he always felt at Koo's detached smile and undercurrent of surliness. "Tom in the office?"

Koo nodded and went back to work.

Matt and Lisa stopped in front of the jaguars' cage.

"They're beautiful," Lisa said.

They certainly did look fine. The larger one, Diego, was pacing back and forth. Rosa lay on the shelf and watched Matt, unblinking.

In his office Tom O'Rourke was busy with a work sheet. Matt introduced Lisa and told Tom she'd like to interview him. "Now's as good a time as any," Tom said. He offered them coffee from a thermos on the desk.

Matt declined. "I'm trying to get through my rounds— little late this morning. Everything all right here?"

"Fine. Awful about Mrs. Winston."

Matt nodded. He looked out the window. There were bars and wire mesh on the large window that overlooked both the lion and tiger enclosures. From here he could see the high chain-link double fences that separated the enclosures from Route 63, which went through the center of Braeton and on to Addison University. When the enclosures were built, before he came to the zoo, many Braeton residents were concerned about their safety because of the lions and tigers on the prowl in open fields. Their fears had been allayed by the double fences and elaborate locks on the gates that were necessary to give access to the enclosures for landscaping and cleaning.

"What do you think of the new jags?" Matt asked.

"She knew how to pick 'em all right." Tom shook his head.

His white hair framed a red-veined drinker's face. He was a wiry man with scars on his face and hands. You couldn't be lucky all the time when you worked with the big cats. Although some people said they could be tamed if you got them young enough, Matt doubted it. Their innate savageness made them unpredictable. He'd discussed this with Jacky many times. She didn't agree. Now he thought, maybe she'd been too trusting, and not only of animals.

"I'll leave you two, then," Matt said. "Tom's got plenty of good stories to tell," he told Lisa.

Matt went into the main exhibit area. It was silent. Koo was gone. The visitors had all moved on. The indoor cages were empty except for the jaguars' cage. The jags would be kept inside for observation for at least another week before they were allowed outdoors. Matt stood in front of the cage again and watched Diego pacing back and forth as if looking for a way out.

Something was troubling Matt about the jags, a memory as shapeless as a shadow. He watched the lithe dappled animal marking the new boundaries of his life and remembered the jags' arrival last Tuesday evening. He hadn't expected them so soon. He'd thought they wouldn't be let out of quarantine until Wednesday. Working late in his office Tuesday night, he'd seen the truck pull up to the gate and knew it must be the jags. By the time he got to the Big Cats House, Jacky, with Koo's help, had already let the animals out of the metal traveling cages into the exhibit cage, and they were uneasily exploring the confines of their new home.

At first Jacky had seemed flustered by Matt's arrival. "I thought you tried not to work nights," she'd said.

When he began to reply, she'd laughed and said, "Anyway, I'm glad you're here to greet them."

Now, as he watched the jags, he remembered that Koo had been there also, in the shadows near the keeper's office.

64

But there was nothing unusual about that. Koo kept odd hours and came and went at will, sometimes even bedded down on the couch in the keeper's office.

The cages the jags had been shipped in were stacked on the floor. He'd offered to call maintenance. "If Charlie's still there, I'll get him to come up. He and Koo can move the cages out of here."

"No," Jacky had said. Did her voice have an edge to it? "Don't trouble yourself. Koo will take care of it."

Matt started to protest, but stopped when Jacky did an astonishing thing: she stood on her tiptoes and kissed him gently on the lips. "Let's celebrate," she said. "Just you and me. After all, this was your idea. We'll stop for a bottle of champagne and drink it at your place. Then you can take me home."

They'd done just that. They'd laughed and talked and drunk the champagne. Since that night she'd been warmer toward him than she'd been for a very long time, as if he were a favorite brother or a close friend. He'd had to work hard not to yearn for her as he'd sworn he'd never allow himself to do again.

Now, standing in front of the jags' cage, he wondered if that sudden renewal of intimacy had started as a ploy to take his mind off the cages.

Just then Rosa leaped soundlessly from the shelf to the floor. The flash of color brought Matt back to the present only seconds before the two-way radio in his pocket began to buzz.

"Matt Yates," he said as Rosa's jewelled eyes watched him.

Addie's voice quavered through the static. "Matt. It's that police lieutenant—Cohen."

"Yes?"

"He'd like you to meet him at Anuk's den."

"When?"

"Now. Right now. He says it's important."

— 12 —

COHEN WAS WAITING for him outside the den. He smiled, arms folded across his chest, as Matt climbed the path toward him.

"That was fast." He always sounded as if he was joking or teasing. Blustery was a good description of his tone, Matt thought. And a good method it was to cover up anything the detective didn't want to reveal.

"I was nearby. At the Big Cats House."

"We're finished here," Cohen said as Matt came up beside him. "You can have the bears moved back whenever you want."

Matt was surprised. "But the heel?"

"We found it. Early this morning." Cohen pointed to the leaves deeply piled beneath the fence around the upper level of the den. "Here."

Matt looked at the many-colored leaves. He saw nothing.

"It's already gone to the lab."

"Well, then." Matt sighed. He felt a stunning relief mixed with sorrow. "So she did fall."

"One would be expected to conclude that." Cohen was scratching his head.

"But you don't?" Matt was confused, but he was already beginning to understand Cohen. He liked to present you with a puzzle. He liked to watch you try to solve it.

"Could we walk over to your office?" Cohen asked.

They started off, Hughes following behind them on the gravel path.

As they passed the tiger enclosure, Raji stood near the edge of the moat and watched them. Matt made the purring sound that the tigers often responded to. Raji purred back, a soft rumbly sound, and continued to watch Matt with his amber eyes.

"Well, look at that," Cohen said. "That tiger is purring at you like a great big pussycat. Are they tame, then?"

Matt laughed. "Tame? Hardly. Responsive is what they are. Sure, he purrs back when I purr to him, as long as he's content, well fed, secure in his quarters and his routine. But he's a wild animal. No amount of so-called civilizing can change that. If he was hungry or if you crossed into his territory, he'd tear you apart." Matt thought of the sight of Jacky's torn body and fell silent.

"A zoo is not such a safe place," Cohen said.

"It is if you follow the rules," Matt replied, holding open the door to the administration building for Cohen and Hughes.

"No calls 'til we're through, please," Matt instructed Addie as he entered his office with the two men.

When they were seated, Hughes took out his notebook. Cohen crossed his legs. "About the heel," he began. Matt sat forward. "It's puzzling. My men found it just where I showed you. But they had looked there yesterday and it wasn't there."

"Maybe they missed it."

"Maybe."

"Didn't you have someone posted to watch the area?" Matt had seen the police car in the parking lot when he left last night and it was still there this morning.

Cohen nodded. "I did. Trouble is, my man admitted he might've dropped off for a bit. So we have a little time gap."

"You think someone sneaked in and left the heel there?"

"Maybe. Or maybe, as you say, we missed it yesterday. The leaves are deep. The rain. Also, if someone sneaked in, how did he get in? My man claims that he slept for only a few minutes at about six o'clock this morning. The only person who entered the zoo before that time was your assistant cats keeper, Eustis Cooney."

"Koo. Hmm."

"It's also possible that someone stayed inside the zoo through the night."

Matt nodded.

"We're checking your gate records further. And I would like you to tell me again about the keys that open the locks on the gates to the lion and tiger enclosures, both the gates from the zoo and the ones from Route 63."

"As I told you, those keys are kept in my safe. I had the locks changed when I took over as director, and the keys are never out of my control. There's no chance that anyone could have made copies of them." Matt thought for a moment, then added, "Besides, no one would enter the enclosures because the lions and tigers go in and out at will. It has to be arranged in advance; the cats rounded up and locked inside their cages before we can let anyone into the enclosures.

"I see." Cohen looked thoughtful.

"So you think someone might've gotten in somehow and waited to see if your policeman dozed off so he could plant that heel?" Matt asked.

Cohen laughed. "You make it sound unlikely. But I think it's possible that someone might've been watching for just such an opportunity, and took it when it occurred. Someone who would much prefer that we think Mrs. Winston climbed up on that fence herself."

"But it could just as easily not have occurred—the opportunity."

"But worth waiting for."

Yes, Matt thought. It would've been worth a try, if you thought that finding the heel now would convince the police it had been there from the start and, therefore, that Jacky had walked up the path on her own two feet. "So you believe that someone watched for an opportunity, then planted the heel?"

"No. I don't believe it. My men could've missed the heel in the leaves yesterday. What I believe is that it's certainly possible someone put it there this morning. I want to find out who could've been in the zoo or gotten into the zoo to do so."

Matt felt Cohen's eyes steadily upon him. He met those eyes, heavy-lidded, deceptively sleepy. Something more was on the man's mind.

"Anyway," Cohen said as if divulging a secret, "it's really strange about those shoes. We found dirt on the bottom of her stocking-feet, which shows she'd taken the shoes off at some point and walked around without them."

Matt looked at him, interested.

"So why did she put them on again?" Cohen asked.

There was a silence in the room. Even the scratching of Hughes's pen stopped. Through the closed door Matt could hear the muffled sound of Addie's typing. He looked expectantly at Cohen, but Cohen was looking at him. What did he want?

"I was waiting for you to tell me about the theft at the zoo," Cohen said pleasantly.

Matt felt his face flush like that of a guilty person. "I just found out about it. I'm still trying to sort it all out. How did you find out?"

Cohen only smiled.

Of course, Cohen would know about the theft. He was interviewing everyone at the zoo, discussing everything that might possibly have a connection to the case.

"There's something else you didn't tell me about," Cohen continued.

"What's that?"

Cohen was watching Matt carefully. "That you and Mrs. Winston had been lovers."

Matt was surprised. He would never have thought of telling Cohen something so personal. It was irrelevant to the present, that brief happy time so long ago. "It didn't seem important. My God, it's been over for twenty years." He stopped himself from adding six months and seventeen days, but he might just as well have said it, the way Cohen was looking at him.

"Over," Cohen repeated, "but not for you."

Matt opened his mouth to speak, closed it again.

"Why don't you just tell me about it," Cohen said.

"There's not much to tell. We met in college—Cornell— in zoology lab. We fell in love. She fell out of love. I didn't. But she loved me—like a friend—and I felt the same about her."

"The same. You mean you loved her like a friend."

"Right."

"But that's not all you felt for her."

"No. I just told you. I was in love with her. From the moment I saw her. That never changed."

"So." Cohen sat still, unsmiling. "She fell out of love with you. When did that occur?"

Matt laughed without mirth. "Almost as soon as she fell in love with me."

70

"She met someone else? John Winston?"

"No, she didn't meet John until years later. It wasn't another man. It was that she just wasn't in love with me." Matt looked down at his hands.

"How did you know that?"

Matt looked up, almost surprised to see himself face to face with the police lieutenant. "She told me. We'd only been going together for a few months when she told me."

"What did she tell you?"

"That she liked me and respected me. That she'd like to be in love with me, but that she knew herself well enough to know that she couldn't be happy with me. She needed a man who was forceful, authoritative . . ." He trailed off.

"Don't sound like the kind of traits that make a good husband."

Matt sighed. "She knew it. She even said that. She said the men she fell in love with always turned out to be bastards. That was why she wanted, she really wanted, to be in love with me."

Cohen said nothing.

"I begged her," Matt continued. "I told her that what she needed was someone who truly loved her, that her need for a tough guy was self-destructive. I begged her to stay with me, to give me a chance." Matt looked out the window, over Hughes's head. He'd never told this story to anyone. It struck him as sad that these two policemen should be his only confidants. "She said I was right, but that's the way she was and she didn't want to hurt me any more than she already had. That it had been a mistake to lead me on and she wouldn't do that anymore. After that it was over. I tried, God knows, I tried for a long time. But over the years I accepted it."

Matt sat up straight. His neck was stiff and he stretched it, trying to loosen up the muscles. He felt as if he were

71

emerging from a deep dive. His ears seemed to ring with the pressure.

"Thank you for your honesty," Cohen said.

Matt sighed, relieved. "Then you believe me."

Cohen nodded, but said, "You should have told me yourself about the theft and about your relationship with Mrs. Winston. Any of these things could be important in our investigation."

Matt thought about that for a moment. "Are you suggesting that the theft at the zoo has something to do with Jacky's death?"

"Think about it," Cohen said. "There are many ways in which it could." He paused. "And think about yourself. Let's assume you're not the guilty party—in either the possible murder or the theft. Both crimes could have been committed by you. Think of that the next time you have any information that might have a bearing on this case." Cohen stood up. "I'm sure we'll have occasion to talk further. Don't bother getting up." He walked out of Matt's office with Hughes at his heels.

Matt continued to sit at his desk, as exhausted as if he had just swum a mile. It had never occurred to him that the theft and Jacky's death could be related. It had certainly never occurred to him to tell Cohen that he and Jacky had been lovers, that Cohen might think that their once being in love could have anything to do with her murder. Who killed Jacky? Who stole from the zoo? Was it the same person? Someone who was trying to set him up?

He started at the knock on his door. Lisa walked in, beaming. "Tom gave me great stuff. Told me about his circus days, his philosophy of training exotic animals. Even showed me his scars. How was your meeting with the police?"

"How did you . . . ?"

"Addie, of course."

Matt shook his head, looking glum. "Bad and it gets worse. Cohen thinks the theft may be related to Jacky's death."

"Cohen! Lieutenant Cohen?"

"You know him?"

"He handled the investigation into the deaths at Addison last year."

"Seems smart."

"Yeah. I think he is," Lisa said grudgingly, remembering his condescending attitude toward her. "So he thinks the theft and Jacky's death could be related."

"Don't you?" Matt asked.

"Sure. And it could be coincidence too."

"And then there's the heel," Matt said as if to himself.

"What heel?"

Matt explained that Jacky's heel had been missing and then found in the leaves this morning.

"So someone could've planted the heel there for the police to find. That what Cohen thinks?"

"Yes. Except no one but Koo was in the zoo at the time."

"And it could've been there all along."

"Could've." Matt paused. "There's something else." Whatever it was, he seemed to find it difficult to tell her. Finally he began, "A long time ago, Jacky and I . . . we . . ." he trailed off, banged his palms down on the desk.

"You were in love."

"Are you psychic or something?"

"Matt, you wore it on your sleeve. I observed you Sunday night at the Gala."

He reddened. "We were friends. Only that. But a long time ago, when we were at Cornell, we were a lot more than that to each other. Not for long, though. She stopped being in love with me. Maybe she never was. But I didn't stop.

73

She was my best friend. The other feelings, I pushed them down. I learned how to deal with them a long time ago."

Lisa nodded. Sure you did, she thought, remembering that expression on his face Sunday night. "So you told Cohen about you and Jacky?"

"He knew. I didn't tell him."

"Why didn't you?"

"I didn't think it was important."

"How did he find out?"

"I don't know exactly. But others knew about it. John Winston did, and you know how gossip spreads in a place like the zoo and, of course, Cohen's questioning everybody."

"You're worried that he's suspicious because you didn't tell him yourself?"

"I don't know. Don't you think he might be?" He looked worried.

Lisa was thoughtful. "Depends. On how his investigation is going, what he's finding out. Maybe you could tell me more about her. When we have more time. Might help."

He sighed and turned toward her. "Sure." He reached across his desk and squeezed her hand. "Thanks."

She felt warmed by his trust in her and remembered the closeness they'd once had. Since then, she'd never had a male friend she could trust the way she'd trusted him. Of course, there had been Sam. But she'd talked to him on the phone only a few times since she left Addison. She hadn't seen him. Funny. In a lot of ways Matt reminded her of Sam. Could it be that she could never appreciate the sweet needy guys who appreciated her? Could be, she thought.

13

"MAYBE you'd rather I left you alone," Koo said.

Johnny sat in the soft white leather chair, his cheek in his hand. "No," he said, watching Koo through dulled eyes. "Don't go."

Koo came over and sat on the arm of Johnny's chair, allowing his leg, clad in slim jeans, to swing, gently bumping Johnny's leg.

Johnny put a hand on Koo's thigh and looked up at him. His expression was piteous. "I loved her," he said, his voice low.

Koo looked down at Johnny. Tears were streaming down his face. Koo covered Johnny's hand with his own.

"I can't believe it," Johnny said in a choked voice. He was quiet for a few moments. "Did I ever tell you about the time she got sick? We were on a hunt in Kenya."

Koo had heard it before. Many times. But he said, "Go on."

"She had a high fever. She thought she was going to die. She told me she loved me. She said, 'I love you, Johnny. I love you.' Nobody'd ever told me that before."

Koo felt a momentary revulsion looking down at Johnny's agonized features. Wouldn't you know he'd be feeling sorry for himself? With his stepmother not even buried yet. "I've told you that—that I loved you," he forced himself to say. He thought about how close love and hate were.

Johnny's face relaxed a little. He didn't seem to notice the past tense. He looked up at Koo, and Koo remembered what he'd fallen for in the first place. Those wide-set blue eyes. Koo remembered the day it had all begun. Last April. He'd been at the zoo for several months, but he'd just started the job of assistant keeper for the big cats. He'd never worked with big cats before, but he told Tom O'Rourke he'd had experience with them in his previous job because he wanted the assistant keeper's job.

But on his first assignment, he was over his head and he knew it. He was trying to get Raji into the holding cage so that he could give him an injection of antibiotics. He had placed a piece of meat in the holding cage and pushed the cage right up against the open door to Raji's sleeping quarters. Then he had stood inside the exhibit cage and called Raji, coaxingly at first, then more and more impatiently as the tiger did not respond to his efforts.

Johnny had walked into the Big Cats House just as Koo lost patience and shouted at the tiger, "Damn you, you evil monster."

Koo heard a laugh and whirled around. There was Johnny, laughing at him. He'd seen Johnny around the zoo and knew him as Winston's son with the cushy PR job, but they'd never spoken.

"Who's the master here," Johnny said, still laughing, "you or that poor dumb brute with the respiratory infection?"

"Well, do it yourself, if you're so fucking smart." Koo banged out of the cage.

"Come on," Johnny said, "Don't be mad. I'm just trying to help."

Johnny had climbed into the exhibit cage then, and stood

76

beside the holding cage, whistling softly, a soothing sing-song tune without melody. Every once in a while he would stop whistling and make a strange sound, a cross between a gargle and a purr. After several minutes of Johnny's sound effects, Koo saw the tawny head of the tiger appear at the door of his sleeping quarters. Johnny purred to him. Raji looked at Johnny, then made an incredible noise in the back of his throat, that seemed like an imitation of Johnny's. They spoke back and forth to each other in this manner and after a while Raji walked on soft paws into the holding cage. He brushed the meat with his nose, then purred at Johnny. Johnny purred back and Raji began to eat.

Johnny let the tiger eat undisturbed, continuing to purr, and every once in a while the tiger would look up from his treat and purr back. Then Johnny began to turn the crank that moved the barred sides of the holding cage closer together. Raji, concentrating on his food, didn't seem to notice until the sides were almost touching him. By then the meat had been eaten and he was no longer distracted. He looked around at Johnny as the sides of the cage moved even closer and pressed into his flanks. Johnny was still purring, but Raji did not answer now. He sensed danger. He tried to push away from the sides of the cage, but could not. He snarled and thrashed, moving his great head back and forth, his fangs bared.

To Koo, standing in front of the exhibit cage, marveling at Johnny's skill, the tiger's snarl and the bared yellow fangs were terrifying.

Johnny, still purring and talking gently to Raji, stopped long enough to say, "Quick, get your hypodermic ready. One more twist of the handle and his left flank will be immobilized."

Koo did as he was told. He leapt into the cage, needle at the ready, and plunged it into the animal's flank. As he did

77

so, Johnny touched the nervous tiger firmly yet gently on the head, talking to him all the while.

Watching Johnny handle Raji, Koo felt as if he, himself, were under Johnny's hands being soothed and cared for.

The injection was over in an instant. And afterward, Johnny had continued to talk to Raji, soothing and explaining while he let him out of the holding cage and back into his sleeping quarters. As the tiger jumped out of the cage, Johnny had patted his side and made that strange sound from puckered lips again. Raji turned and looked at Johnny with eyes that shone like copper pennies and purred back. All is forgiven. As if he knew that the injection had been for his own good.

That afternoon was the first time Koo had heard a tiger purr. And although he had often purred to his tigers since and they had often purred back, he'd never lost the sense of Johnny's mastery, of his assurance with animals. It was an impression that had stayed with Koo and had turned into a belief in Johnny's power over animals in an almost magical way. Koo was convinced that Johnny could communicate with animals in a way other humans couldn't. When after work that day, Johnny had shown up at the Big Cats House and they'd gone out for a beer and then back to Johnny's apartment, he'd felt drawn to Johnny. More than he'd ever been to anyone before.

Koo had been impressed with the deep Oriental rugs, the white leather furniture as soft as flesh, and the apartment house itself, on the hill overlooking the zoo and the Boston skyline beyond, like a band of jewels in the nighttime distance. Johnny had money and he was generous with it. He bought Koo presents, took him out to fancy restaurants, even wanted him to move in to this posh apartment with him. Koo knew when he was well off.

But despite Johnny's strength with animals, there was something weak about his nature that Koo was finding more and more annoying. In fact, Koo himself was the one with the power. And the more he got the upper hand, the more contempt he felt for Johnny.

It had happened to him before. His last relationship, before he came north, with an insurance salesman in St. Crail, had taken the same path. Now, as he sat holding Johnny's hand and wishing he were someplace else, he wondered if there was a pattern to it.

Johnny looked up at him again, wiping his eyes. "You really mean it?" he asked.

"What?" Koo was jolted from his thoughts.

"You really love me?"

"I'm moving in, aren't I?" What does he want? Koo thought, willing the impatience out of his eyes as Johnny watched him carefully. "Why do you keep asking?"

"Because," Johnny began, "because Jacky told me. After the Gala she told me about . . ."

Goddamn. Koo's heart was pounding. "What did she tell you?" he asked as calmly as he could.

"About you and her. She told me about how you were lovers."

What did she have to do that for? Koo cursed to himself. What'd she have to try to destroy what I have? But it could've been worse, and he knew it. At least she didn't tell Johnny the secret he'd once told her. She'd been so tender to him, he'd wanted to tell her. It had felt so good to tell her, to get it off his chest. But right after, he'd been sorry. "Look, it wasn't important," he said.

Johnny was waiting.

"It happened right after I started here at the zoo and it didn't last very long."

Johnny said nothing.

"She was really unhappy. She'd had a big fight with your father. She was thinking of getting out."

"Yeah. That was when she first found out about Mariel."

"About who?"

"Mariel McCabe. That anchorwoman from WQTE. She found out my father'd been screwing her."

"So?"

Johnny's fists were clenched. "He'd been faithful for a while. She thought things were better. Then she finds out he's fucking that dish—everybody's leftovers. It changed her."

Koo felt relieved. Johnny was handing him a great excuse. "Yeah, well that's when it happened, with us I mean. I didn't even know you. All I knew about her was that she was Winston's wife. So one day I'm filling the pool outside the Elephant House and she comes over and asks me to go out for a drink with her."

"I thought you didn't go for women."

"I didn't. Don't. But she was different. Not clingy and whiny. She just went after what she wanted."

"You."

"Me. But only because she was mad. I was like a way of getting it out of her system."

"You liked it," Johnny accused.

Koo looked away, out the window at a television antenna somewhere out there near Boston, winking red in the blackness. "It wasn't good," he said softly, aware of the fineness of his own profile, the gold hair in his eyes, aware of Johnny's eyes on him. "Like I told you before, it's never been good for me with a woman." He could feel Johnny relax beside him. "And then I met you," he finished simply.

Johnny reached up and pulled Koo down beside him on the big soft chair. Johnny had started to cry again. He held Koo tightly, his cheek pressed to Koo's cheek, and Koo could taste the salt of Johnny's tears. "She was trying to make me give you up, trying to tell me you couldn't be trusted and

80

that I shouldn't let you move in. And something more," Johnny said, his voice childlike through the tears.

Koo was gripped by panic again. So she *had* told him. "What? What did she tell you?"

Johnny hesitated. "She . . . she started to . . . Nothing," he said finally. "Nothing."

Koo realized he was holding his breath. He let it out in a sudden rush. Thank God, he said to himself. Thank God that's all she told him.

Johnny's tears had stopped. He pressed his lips to Koo's and put his arms around him. Johnny's breath smelled like butterscotch. Koo closed his eyes and relaxed into Johnny's arms. He tasted sweetness and salt. He felt Johnny's strong fingers stroking him. He didn't have to think anymore.

14

COHEN GOT IN early Wednesday morning. He was humming as he hung up his jacket. He sat at his desk looking through papers.

It was a little after eight thirty when Hughes arrived, a large brown envelope under his arm. He tipped its contents out onto Cohen's desk. "They weren't finished at the lab when I got there, so I had to wait," he said. He leaned over Cohen's desk.

Cohen picked up the photographs one at a time. John Winston. Alden Vining. Matthew Yates. John Winston, Jr. Jacky Winston. George Finn. Susan Neiman. He smiled. "Better. Much better." Then he stacked them in a pile, like a deck of cards, and slid them back into the envelope. He got up and took his jacket from the coat rack, smoothing it over his shoulder holster as he put it on.

Hughes was grinning. Enlarging the photographs had been his idea. The portraits in the annual B.Z.S. bulletin had been small, too small to identify readily, they'd decided when they looked at them yesterday afternoon. Besides, in the bulletin, each photograph was identified with name and position. Now they were nameless.

Cohen handed the envelope to Hughes. "Let's go."

Hughes drove east on the Mass Turnpike and got off at the Newton exit. Cohen was quiet during the drive, and Hughes glanced over at him several times. His boss seemed lost in thought. Hughes knew better than to disturb him. He would've liked to open a window, but then Cohen would probably start to sneeze. Better to be hot than responsible for his boss's allergy attack, Hughes thought.

The Center Street traffic was stop and go. It was still rush hour. In Newton Center Hughes parked beside a no-parking sign in front of MassColony Bank and turned to Cohen. "Funny the embezzler used this bank to deposit and cash his checks. It's kind of out of the way, isn't it?"

"Not if you live in Newton Center," Cohen said, easing himself out of the car.

Hughes was beside him on the sidewalk. "Well, of course, but none of our suspects does." He opened the bank's door for Cohen, who turned to him with a smile and said, "I think we'll find that's exactly why he—or she—used this bank, because no one knows him here. He wouldn't be recognized. He would hope that he wouldn't even be noticed. We, of course, hope that he was—noticed, that is."

Hughes flashed a look of admiration that made Cohen smile again. Not a bad assistant. A little dense, perhaps, but not bad at all.

They entered the bank lobby that, although busy, was as quiet as a library. Cohen showed his ID to the pale young man who came toward him. "Manager, please," Cohen said.

They were shown into a small glass cubicle. A portly man with rimless glasses was closing a folder and shaking his head as they entered. "Our manager, Mr. Jennings," the pale man said and returned to his post.

Cohen explained the purpose of their visit.

83

"Well," Mr. Jennings said, shaking his head again. "A.C.E. Grain. Let us see." He pressed the keys of the computer on his desk delicately with two pointer fingers. In a moment green glowing letters and figures filled the screen.

Cohen and Hughes watched.

Jennings pointed at the screen. "This date shows us when A.C.E. Grain opened the account—May thirty first."

"Two weeks after the first requisition," Cohen said to Hughes. Cohen pointed to the screen, "And this is the name of the person who opened the account?"

"Yes. Henry A. Smith."

"Could you describe him?"

"I didn't see him, as far as I know," Jennings said. "He could've opened the account through any of our customer representatives." He waved toward the row of desks outside his office.

Cohen was examining the numbers on the screen.

"These are deposits," Jennings explained, pointing to a list of figures on the left. Moving his finger to the right, he said, "Withdrawals. And after each transaction we have the date and a code for the place where the transaction took place."

Cohen looked closely. "Okay, that first transaction, on May thirty first, took place at NC. What's NC—this bank?"

"Right. NC is Newton Center. Other branches are represented by different initials."

"I see that many of the subsequent deposits have L St as the location. What's that?"

"That's one of our electronic banking terminals—on Leonard Street, not far from here, in the mall."

"And you can make a deposit there?"

"Surely. You just insert the check or cash in a deposit envelope."

Cohen studied the screen. "And the withdrawals are marked L St except for a few larger ones marked NC."

"That's right. Our electronic terminals will give up to three hundred and fifty dollars. For a larger withdrawal you must go to the bank."

Cohen pointed to the last withdrawal, an NC. "The last withdrawal is for exactly what was in the account."

"Yes. Seems to have closed it out on October fifth."

"October fifth. That date tell you something, Hughes?" Cohen asked.

"Uhmmm . . ."

"Never mind. Later." Cohen turned back to Jennings. "I'd like to speak to your customer representatives and tellers."

Cohen felt a rising of hope as he followed Jennings out of his office. Ten minutes later his hope was dashed. Not one of the six bank employees he'd spoken to recognized the account of A.C.E. Grain or remembered a man named Henry A. Smith who had started the account last May. Cohen showed each of them the photographs, but none responded to any of them, except for Daphne Shecter, a teller who said of John Winston that he strongly resembled her uncle Max.

"Is it unusual that they don't remember?" Cohen asked.

"I don't think so," Jennings said. "Our customer volume is quite large."

"I'll let you know if there's any more activity in the account," Jennings promised.

"Thank you. I doubt it'll be necessary," Cohen said, but he left his card with Jennings just in case.

Standing in front of the bank with an envelope containing copies of the computer printout of A.C.E.'s account and the card Henry Smith filled out, Cohen was disappointed.

The Newton Center post office was a short walk from the bank. There was a line inside. Cohen stepped around it and showed his ID to the clerk. The clerk motioned them to the door and called out as they entered, "Office on your left. Ask for Tom Grinnell."

In the office a man sat at a desk shooting the breeze with some other men who were sitting on top of his desk. They were laughing and drinking Cokes.

Looks like nice work, Cohen thought, but boring as hell. "Tom Grinnell?" he asked, holding out his ID. The others got up off the desk and ambled out of the office.

Cohen told Grinnell about the A.C.E. post office box. Grinnell looked up the form in his files. Henry Smith had come into the Newton Center post office on May seventeenth, the very day of the first requisition, and ordered the box. His signature on the form looked very much like the signature on the bank card.

"We'd like an identification of him," Cohen said. "We have photographs here. What we need to find out is which of your postal clerks could have been at the desk when Mr. Smith filled out the card.

"May," Grinnell said thoughtfully. "I'll take you around. Introduce you to the crew."

Cohen went through his routine with the three clerks who took turns manning the desk. None of them remembered. None could identify any of the photos.

"Damn," Cohen cursed under his breath.

After their last interview, Cohen poked his head in at Grinnell's door. A few men were back in the office, joking loudly. "Mr. Grinnell," Cohen interrupted. "That's it, then? We've seen everyone who might have been on the desk when Mr. Smith applied for the box?"

Grinnell nodded. "That's it."

"Hey, what about Jim Fontaine?" a man with a red beard asked.

Grinnell slapped a hand to his head. "Jim. Son of a gun. He could've been on the desk in May."

"Where can I reach him?" Cohen asked.

"Can't. He's on his honeymoon."

"He'd never dare tell us where that was," redbeard said. The others laughed.

"He'll be in Monday morning at eight."

"I wouldn't count on it," another said, and they laughed again.

"Eight, Monday," Grinnell said.

Cohen nodded. "Thanks."

Walking back to the car, Hughes asked, "So do we start the financial investigation on all of them?"

Cohen sighed. "Might as well. Can't afford to waste any more time." Disappointed, he shook his head. "Sometimes the easy way works. If you're lucky."

15

LISA STRAIGHTENED the sofa pillows and began to gather the pages of the Sunday *Globe* that were scattered over the sofa and floor. She stacked the paper neatly on the glass coffee table, then went into the bedroom to get ready.

She stepped out of her jeans and flipped them with her toe onto the unmade bed. As she opened the accordion doors of her closet, the left door stuck on the track as usual. She pulled hard and the door lurched off the track with a screech. Damn. She'd have to call the super to fix it again; she'd have to put up with his suggestive talk and unclever jokes. "No," she said, "I'll try it myself. Later." She wriggled into a pair of black tights and stepped into the low heeled black pumps standing among the dust balls on the closet floor.

She tented her denim skirt over her head. It slid down comfortably, an old friend with a flounce at the bottom. She opened the top drawer of the chest and found some gold hoops among the tangle of gold and silver and bright-colored beads. She closed the drawer, then opened it again and took out a turquoise necklace.

She picked up her brush from the top of the chest and absently pulled out the long dark hairs as she watched her reflection in the mirror. She still recognized herself as the girl she'd always been. But she was thirty-one years old. Shouldn't she look like a woman now? Shouldn't she be somehow different? Grown up? I am a woman hiding out in teenagers' clothing, she thought. But as suddenly as it had come the feeling disappeared. This is who I am, she thought. But she still watched herself warily.

She turned from the mirror and surveyed her room: the jeans tosed on the bed, the orange peels and half-full coffee cups on the night table, the dust everywhere. She picked up the jeans and flung them into the closet. She smoothed the quilt over the bed and carried the orange peels and coffee cups into the kitchen.

In the living room she sat on the sofa and looked out the window. Fluffy clouds hung above the buildings in the distance. The sky was a bright hard blue. Sunday afternoon. How many Sunday afternoons had she spent at home with her newspapers after her morning run along the Charles River? Most of her old girlfriends were married now. And those who weren't were trying hard to be.

Lisa sighed. This was the age of women's liberation. She was suppposed to feel free and be happy about it. She did. For the most part. Just every once in a while . . . She thought about the weekend she'd just spent. Yesterday, after her run, she'd done her errands and shopping and then had dinner at her friend Sonia Janis's apartment on Beacon Hill. Sonia's husband Fred and another couple had been merry and friendly, but she'd left with an ache just under her rib cage.

Friday after work she'd gone out for a drink with Sally and Irma who worked in the advertising department of the *Times*. Saleswomen, both of them. Sally, heavily made-up, with dark restless eyes, was divorced and in her late thirties. Irma, in her mid-twenties, polished and intelligent, had straight blond hair and a runner-slim body. While Lisa nursed her one Amstel light, the others drank Stolys straight. The talk shifted from work itself to office gossip, then, inevitably, to "Men".

Sally, the authority by dint of her experience, spoke of the impossibility of the union of an ambitious woman with any male of the species. "Their goddamned egos." She rolled her eyes toward the bar where several of "them" sat casing the room. "It's I, I, I or nothing." She sipped the colorless liquid with ease.

Irma laughed. "I had this boyfriend once. He wouldn't let me out of his sight. I began to feel we were handcuffed together, as if I was on my way to jail."

"And now?" Lisa asked.

"Now?"

"You have a boyfriend now?"

"Oh, Dirk." Irma brightened. "He's at Columbia Law School. It really helps being in different cities."

Sitting on her sofa now, Lisa thought she had a pretty good idea how Sally and Irma felt about "Men", but she was as confused as ever about how she felt. So far none of her relationships had led to anything permanent. She supposed the most promising had been Sam Harrison, a much older professor at Addison. A decent man, but she hadn't been in love with him.

Her mother was so eager for her to marry. Lisa smiled as she thought of how Anxious Anna used to call her every Sunday morning with her hopeful, "So, anything new?" When, finally, Lisa asked her to stop, her mother pretended she didn't know what she was doing wrong. But she stopped.

Lisa went into the kitchen, washed the coffee cups and ground up the orange peels in the disposal. I just want to be myself, she thought, and if a man comes along who's right for me, good. If not, that's fine too. She nodded her head for emphasis. But she remembered how lost she'd felt after Mickey left her. She didn't want to feel that way again, ever.

90

She was looking out the kitchen window thinking about Absent Abe when she saw Matt parking his battered Vista Cruiser station wagon in the lot. He walked toward the building, his long legs moving like a runner's in a graceful rhythm. Lisa had tried to reach him several times since Tuesday. She'd left messages at his office, but he hadn't returned her calls. On Wednesday she'd dropped in after she talked with Hugo Tollich. But Addie had told her Matt was at a meeting. She'd left a note asking him to call and reminding him about Anna's dinner. And the next day Addie had called to tell her that Matt said he hadn't forgotten and he'd pick her up.

Her bell buzzed and she pressed the button that opened the downstairs door. Then she went to the top of the stairs and called down, "Come on up and see my place before we go."

He took the stairs two at a time, yet arrived at her door unwinded.

"You're a runner," she greeted him.

"You too?" he said with exaggerated surprise.

"Who isn't?"

Matt walked around the living room. He could do it in three steps. "Nice," he said.

Lisa watched him explore the small kitchen. He looked out at the balcony. "Good view."

"There's more." She showed him the bedroom and bathroom.

"All this and running water too," he joked, standing in the tiny bathroom.

In the living room, she realized that there was nothing to sit on but the sofa. "I'm getting some chairs, as soon as I get a raise."

"Hey, I like it this way. Uncluttered, like a Japanese house. You could get those big pillows."

"I've wanted to talk to you all week," Lisa said as they left her apartment.

91

"I'm sorry. I got your messages, but I didn't have even a minute to call you back. It was an awful week."

"The funeral?"

He nodded. "And Cohen's been on my back every day. My phone's going like crazy. Everybody wants to know what's going on." He laughed. "Especially me."

As soon as they were in the car, Lisa blurted out the questions that had been growing since he told her about the theft. "You think Jacky might've known who was stealing money from the zoo? Maybe threatened to tell?"

"I've thought of that."

"Could she have been the thief?"

Matt shook his head. "She had everything money could buy."

"Everything?"

"Hmm. Well, money can't buy happiness, we know. But I never thought she was really unhappy."

"What do you mean, 'really unhappy'?"

"She and John, her husband, they had their problems. He wasn't faithful. But he needed her."

Lisa thought of what she'd seen at the Gala. John had kept his arm around Jacky's waist, had treated her with care as if she were a valuable Meissen vase, but the look in his eyes had been cold. "So he was playing around?"

Matt nodded. "She said he had been for years."

"What about her?"

"She didn't tell me much about that. But I know there have been men."

Lisa wondered how upsetting those men of hers were to Matt. He gave no clue. He was looking straight ahead, apparently concentrating on his driving. She decided not to pursue it further for now.

Climbing the stairs to Anna's apartment, they raced each other. He was ahead, of course, his legs were twice as long as hers. On the second floor landing, he waited for her. When she came up beside him, trying to control her panting with deep breaths, he said, "Thanks, Lisa. I feel much better. It's good to have you to talk to." She put her arm through his and they walked up the last flight together.

Anna hugged Matt and then hugged him again. She could hardly bring herself to let him go. She cried—for Stella, for Harry, for all they had lost. She cried for sorrow, and she cried for happiness. He held her by the shoulders and looked at her. "You look amazing," he said.

She gave Matt her gifts of love—golden chicken soup, flecked with green dill, in which carrot wheels swam beside glistening noodles, pot roast so tender it crumbled at a fork's touch, browned potatoes with crackly crust. She watched him eat, nodding her head with pleasure at each forkful he carried to his mouth. And for a skinny man, Matt's performance was astonishing.

Lisa, elbows on the table beside her piled plate, watched the drama being played out—Anna giving love, Matt receiving it. And she felt she was relearning something about him, something she had known as a child, something about his capacity for love.

"I should've come to see you sooner," he said to Anna, pushing away his empty plate.

Anna knew better than to offer thirds. She nodded. "Now you'll come." The tone of her voice, mimicking her shtetl ancestors, told all. It was a combination of commanding and pleading with a touch of humor in the questioning quaver at the end of the phrase.

Matt laughed. "You've got yourself a regular."

On the way back to Cambridge, Lisa started her questions again. "Can you think of anyone who would've wanted Jacky dead?"

"I can't. But I don't really know that much about her private life."

"Why don't you tell me what you do know. Start with her husband. Is he her first?"

"John. He's the first. The only. When she married him, they were crazy about each other."

"When was that?"

"About thirteen years ago. I'd just started at the Worcester Zoo. Jacky was in Boston, trying to make a go of her camera safari business."

"Wasn't he a lot older?"

"Twenty years. But when she met him, she told me she'd finally found the man she could love. Only one little trouble—he was already married."

"What happened?"

"He gave the wife a lot of money to get out of his life."

"Jacky didn't feel guilty about taking a married man away from his wife?"

"I doubt it."

Lisa shook her head. "No guilt, hmm."

"That's the way she was. She was fair."

Lisa started to laugh.

"What I mean is, she was fair by her own lights," Matt explained.

"Which means?"

Matt was thinking. "I guess what I mean is she was very sure of herself. If she thought something was right—right for herself, or just the way things should be—she'd go after it. . . ." He stopped.

"No matter what?" Lisa finished.

Matt pulled up in front of Lisa's building. "I truly don't know how far she'd go."

"The theft," Lisa said, knowing he was thinking about it too. "Would she go as far as that?"

"But why would she steal? Fifty or sixty grand. She's got jewels worth more than that."

"Maybe she'd incurred a big expense," Lisa suggested. "Gambling debt? Something like that?"

Matt shook his head. "She got her kicks out of big game hunts, breeding rare cats at her ranch."

"What happened to the camera safari business?"

"Oh, that was before she married John. That's how she earned her living. And that's how she met him. He signed on. They fell madly in love watching a leopard stalk an impala from their blind. She was so sure about him."

"And you weren't?"

"I knew as soon as I met him what an arrogant son of a bitch he was. But it took her a lot longer to find that out."

"So she was happy with him for a while."

"She was happy until he started pawing other women. Then it was all downhill."

"Why didn't she leave him?"

"Good question. I don't really know. I think they made their peace, kind of went their own way. In all honesty, he wasn't bad to her. He liked her. He wanted her around. The zoo was very important to both of them." Matt paused. "And then there was Johnny. A strange guy ever since I've known him. But he and Jacky were very close. He's only a few years younger than she is."

"What do you mean 'strange'?"

"Oh, he was always a sullen, rebellious kid with a terrible temper. Couldn't stick it at school or at any job. One of those kids who bad-mouth their fathers yet seem totally dependent on them. John Winston was always bailing him out of something. Finally, he got Johnny the job as PR person here at the zoo."

"And what kind of relationship did Johnny and Jacky have?"

"She was very protective of him."

"And he?"

"I think he really loved her. And they spent a lot of time together. They've gone on several hunts for exotic animals for the zoo together."

"And how did Winston feel about the relationship between Jacky and Johnny?"

"From what I could see, he was grateful to Jacky. He thought she was helping Johnny. And I believe she was."

"So you don't think Jacky and Johnny could have been having an affair."

"No chance. Johnny's gay, and I guess everyone knows about it but his father."

"Gay? How do you know that?"

"Jacky told me."

Lisa was thoughtful. Then she asked, "Did Johnny go with her on the hunt for the jaguars?"

"No. Not this time. I don't know why, but he didn't."

"Why did she want to get the jaguars? Did you want them?"

"We had talked about it, and I thought it was a good idea. They'll soon be extinct in South America, what with the population expansion into jungle areas and the natives killing them. She wanted to breed them. It was one of her pet projects—breeding cats at her ranch. You know, speaking of the jaguars, there's something that's been bothering me."

"What's that?"

"The evening they arrived, I went over to look at them. Their cages, the ones they'd been transported in, were on the floor in front of the exhibit cage. I offered to call the service department to have the cages picked up and taken to the storehouse. Jacky's reaction seemed odd to me, as if she didn't want those cages touched. I didn't think much about it at the time. But the more I think about it, the stranger it seems."

96

"You think there was something about the cages she didn't want you to see?"

"Maybe. I felt I had surprised her. The jags had come in a day earlier than I'd expected. Maybe I was wrong, but I had the feeling she didn't want me around." He paused, remembering, his frown deepening. "Yet she was warm to me, warmer than she'd been in a long time. At the time, I had the fleeting thought that she was trying to distract me from the cages."

"Maybe so."

"But then I decided that she was warm because she was happy. She told me she was in love."

"Did she say with whom?"

Matt shook his head. "She didn't say. She just asked me to keep it a secret and said she'd tell me more when she could."

"Do you think she was planning to leave her husband?"

"She didn't say that, but I had the feeling she was going to change her life—or thought she could, anyway."

"And after that evening how did she seem to you?"

"I didn't see much of her. When I did, she seemed happy, happier than she'd been, I'd say. And the night of the Gala she seemed positively ecstatic."

Lisa nodded. She'd thought so too. She remembered the energy and joy that had radiated from Jacky Winston when she talked about the jaguars.

"Want to come up for a drink?" Lisa asked when they got to her building.

"Thanks, but I usually stop in at the zoo Sunday afternoon just to check with the keepers, and I want to look in on Solomon, see how his toothache is."

"Give him my love." Lisa leaned over and kissed Matt on the cheek before she got out.

"Could you come for lunch tomorrow?" Matt asked. "I'd

97

like to ask around, see if I can find out where the cages are. I think you could help."

"I can get there around noon. That okay?"

"See you then."

She had a comfortable feeling as she watched him drive off. Not so alone. Growing up it had been just she and Anna alone in the world, taking care of each other, except for that period when the Yateses were a part of their lives. Having Matt back was like having a family again.

16

MATT WAS JUST BEGINNING to make some headway with the papers on his desk Monday morning when Addie poked her head in. "It's those policemen—Lieutenant Cohen and Officer Hughes," she said with a puzzled frown.

Matt sighed and pushed away the stack of architects' drawings for redesigning the space in the old Primates Building.

"And Mr. Vining is with them," Addie finished.

They were right behind her and entered as she stepped back. Alden stood between the two policemen, his head bent so that the line of his aristocratic nose was in shadow. He was dressed impeccably, as always, in a pin-striped suit that was nearly black and shoes shining like money.

Matt stood up in surprise. He turned to Cohen for an explanation. "Mr. Vining asked to have a word with you before we go down to headquarters," Cohen said.

Alden's voice was shaky. "Could you leave us alone?" he asked Cohen.

"I'm sorry, I can't do that." Cohen stood in front of the door.

"Here, sit down," Matt said to Alden, ignoring the policemen. "What's this all about?"

"It's about me. Your thief. Fingered by a guy at the post

office where I took out a box in the name of A.C.E. Grain." He laughed, a harsh, tearing sound. "But for him, I'd have gotten away with it."

"Doubtful," Cohen interposed.

Alden looked at Cohen and said, "It's a relief to have it over, in any case." Then he sank into the chair opposite Matt. "I'm sorry," he said. "I'm the one who's caused you all this trouble with the zoo funds. And I'm sorry."

"You?" Matt couldn't believe it. Alden was rich. He had founded one of the most successful software companies in the area. "But why?"

Alden laughed again, his laugh close to a sob. "For the same reason every other thief steals. I needed the money."

"But Isotech is a huge success."

"Yes. But I ran into a little problem."

"What do you mean?" Matt asked. Then he glanced over at Cohen, who was rocking on his heels, arms folded across his chest. "Look," he said to Alden, "you shouldn't be talking this way. Call your lawyer. Don't say anything more."

Alden waved away the advice. "I've already called my lawyer. He's meeting us at headquarters. I've told him I want to tell everything that happened. I especially want to tell you. Last year I borrowed to develop some hot new software programs. The debts came due and I didn't have the cash. But it was temporary. I was going to pay it all back." Alden leaned forward and fixed Matt with even, gray eyes. "It was only a cash flow problem. I knew I'd have the money well before the end of December for the end of year audit. I was going to put it all back, get rid of the requisition copies in your office and accounting so that no one would notice, but then this damn special audit came up."

"Couldn't you have borrowed more?"

"I suppose, but I felt I was only borrowing the money from the zoo and that it wouldn't be missed."

100

Matt felt a surge of anger, remembering how humiliated he'd felt in front of that group in Winston's office. Then he felt sorry for Alden. "I think you've said enough," he warned.

Alden looked away. There were tears in his eyes when he said, "I don't give a damn. Nothing's any good anymore. I loved her."

Matt closed his eyes. When he opened them, he saw Alden slumped in his chair, head in his hands. Matt pictured her again, as he'd last seen her, the lifeless eyes gazing up to heaven.

"She was going to leave him," Alden said in a husky voice. "But only if I had the means. Don't you see? I needed it—for her. She couldn't live like a pauper. Not Jacky."

"But she was rich. Those diamonds alone."

"As long as she remained his wife, she was rich. If she left him, she gave up everything, including the diamonds."

Matt stared at him, incredulous.

"She'd agreed," Alden explained. "She'd actually signed an agreement. If she left him—nothing."

Matt was surprised that Jacky would have been penniless if she left John. But so what, if they loved each other, she and Alden, why couldn't they make a go of it? She could work—she had before. He could sell off some of his holdings.

"You know how she lived," Alden said, placating. He held his palms out before him.

Sadly, Matt nodded. Alden might be right. Even though Jacky loved him, would she give it all up for him? Her exotic animal hunts, her breeding ranch, her clothes and jewels. Yes. Alden might be right about Jacky's needs. Or, maybe he just didn't dare test her.

"And how did Jacky feel about your salvaging your cash flow by milking the zoo's assets?"

Alden was shocked. His slack face tightened. "Oh, God. I

101

never told Jacky. You know Jacky. You know how she would've felt about anything that threatened the zoo in any way."

"So she didn't know about this cash flow problem of yours then? As far as she knew you were rich?"

"Oh, no. Of course not. I wouldn't have lied to Jacky. I would never have let her give up everything for me."

"What did you tell her?" Matt asked impatiently.

"That I had a money problem, that I hoped I could solve it."

"Hoped!" Matt shouted. "You just told me your problem would be solved by year-end, that if it weren't for the special audit no one would know you'd 'borrowed' money from the zoo."

"Right. Cash flow. Simply . . ." Alden muttered.

"Wait a minute," Matt was angry. "If your money problem was so simple—just a temporary cash flow problem, you could've borrowed, using your shares in the company as collateral."

"All right," Alden snapped. "I wasn't sure I could swing it. But by God I was giving it my all."

Yeah, Matt thought, at my expense. He said, "It was only last month that you bought the Cessna."

Alden looked down at his hands. "She wanted me to teach her to fly."

Matt thought of Alden's houses—the townhouse on Beacon Hill, the spread on Martha's Vineyard and, reputedly, a villa on St. Bart's. Then he thought of Lorna Quentin, her fragile, anxious expression. "Lorna," he said.

Alden looked down at his hands again. "I'm not proud of that. If it weren't for her condition, I couldn't have done it."

Cohen cleared his throat. "Well, we got to get over to my office." He pulled up his pants, which had slipped down under his belly. "We'll talk more later," he said to Matt.

102

Alden put his hand out to Matt. "No matter what happens, I want you to know I'm sorry to cause you trouble. I wanted her. I've never wanted anyone the way I wanted her. I was afraid I'd lose her."

Matt could understand that. A wave of sympathy overcame his disgust and he nodded, allowing his hand to be shaken. He said nothing. All he could think about was Jacky.

As soon as they'd gone, he sat down and swiveled his chair toward the window. Beyond the path in the tiger enclosure Raji was gnawing on a bone. The sight of the healthy animal didn't give him pleasure as it usually did. Cohen and Hughes must suspect that Jacky's death was related to the theft, he thought. After all, they were homicide cops investigating her death. They were the ones who could find out if Alden had had anything to do with it.

He knew why they'd allowed, even encouraged Alden to say his piece—after advising him of his rights, no doubt. They must've learned a lot. Matt certainly had. He'd learned something he'd never even dreamed of. Jacky needed money. He'd also learned that Alden's business was on the brink of failure.

So Jacky needed money. She'd have nothing if she left John. Alden had told her he was in deep financial trouble, but not about the theft from the zoo. Jacky was a woman of action, not one to sit and whine over her bad luck, and for her, no money would be bad luck indeed. Would she sit back, waiting and hoping her beloved would overcome his "cash flow problem" and start making bucks again so she could leave John and live happily ever after with him? Not Jacky. She'd do something. But what?

"I don't know," Matt said aloud, still watching Raji tearing at the bone.

"I like that," a voice behind him said. "So much better

103

than those know-it-all guys who walk around saying 'I know it all.' I knew one like that once."

Matt turned. Lisa was standing in the doorway. She sat down in the chair Alden Vining had just vacated. "Out with it," she said. "I saw your visitors getting into a police car in the parking lot."

"How'd you know they were my visitors?"

"I pulled it out of Addie. Before I persuaded her that you wouldn't mind my coming in unannounced."

Matt shook his head. Then he told her about all that had taken place. "I'm wondering if their need for money had anything to do with Jacky's death. I was thinking about her hunt in Brazil. If she'd sold those jags that she and John gave to the zoo, she could've made a large sum of money."

"But she wouldn't sell them, would she?"

"No. John financed her expeditions. He'd never allow her to sell the animals she captured. Giving animals to the zoo gave him stature, especially when they were captured by his beautiful and daring young wife."

"Unless she sold animals without his consent," Lisa put in.

"Hmm." Matt sat back and thought about that.

"Could she have brought back some other animals along with the jags, secretly, sold them and pocketed the profit."

"Maybe. But what could that possibly have to do with her death?"

"If she did it and John found out, he'd be angry, right?"

"Sure. He wouldn't want to bankroll her business venture so she could make the money to leave him. Besides, he'd think it would be bad for his reputation as the Great Philanthropist."

"He's not going to kill for that, unless the guy's a psychopath. Would he have murdered her if he found out she was planning to leave him?"

"Unlikely. Her leaving wouldn't have cost him financially because of the prenuptial agreement, and, clearly, he wasn't in love with her anymore."

"Maybe he wasn't in love with her, but I saw the way he looked at her the night of the Gala. Possessive. Maybe he'd rather see her dead than lose her."

Matt shook his head. "I can't see that. Unless, as you said, he's crazy."

"He could be crazy."

Matt said nothing.

"Then there's Alden Vining."

"He could've killed her. If so, I think he'll tell Cohen everything, lawyer or not. He was babbling away in here. Who knows what he's capable of?"

"Yes," Lisa said softly, seeing Matt's pain. "It's endlessly fascinating what human beings are capable of."

"Endlessly horrifying."

Lisa started. She'd been thinking of love. "So. Where do we go from here?"

"The cages. I keep coming back to the cages."

He turned and looked out the window. Lisa followed his gaze. One of the tigers was stalking something. Its body low to the ground, it moved swiftly, silently toward its prey, an agent of death.

Lisa recited:

> *"Tiger! Tiger! burning bright*
> *In the forests of the night,*
> *What immortal hand or eye,*
> *Dare frame thy fearful symmetry?"*

"There's a 'fearful symmetry' to this situation, all right. More like an O. Henry story than Blake, though," Matt said, watching the tigers. "If Alden and Jacky were each trying

105

to get money so they could have each other, think of the irony of it! If they'd just accepted each other as they were, rich or poor, Alden wouldn't have stolen and Jacky probably would be alive."

Lisa nodded agreement and got up. "Why don't we go over to the Big Cats House now and see if we can find out anything about the cages?"

The tigers, tired out, were lying sleepily in their enclosure as Matt and Lisa walked by.

"Did he really love her?" Lisa asked.

"I think he did," Matt said, remembering Alden's eyes when he said, "I never wanted anyone the way I wanted her."

"But who is he, anyway? Is he capable of destroying her if he thought he'd lose her? Maybe she was getting tired of him."

Matt shook his head. "I don't know."

17

INSIDE the Big Cats House several visitors were standing in front of the jaguars' cage. Matt and Lisa joined them and watched the jaguars pacing the length of their cage on silent paws.

"They look like they want out," Lisa said.

"They'll go into their own private enclosure as soon as they've settled in a bit longer," Matt explained.

Lisa looked into another cage where a lean spotted cat with a small head was stretching. "Cheetah," she read on the plaque attached to the cage. "Endangered. *Acinonyx jubatus*. Africa. Just one?" she asked.

"We have a pair. But cheetahs are solitary animals. They won't mate if kept together. This is the female, Marika. The male is out in their private enclosure. We introduce Dakar into Marika's cage when she's in estrus, but so far no go." He was silent for a moment, then said, "Jacky was particularly interested in breeding cats."

Koo looked up from his work in one of the cages. His blue eyes had the same magnetic quality as the jaguars' eyes.

"How's it going, Koo?" Matt asked.

"No problem."

"Tom?"

"In the office." Koo gestured toward the door.

Tom was eating a sandwich at his desk, a newspaper propped in front of him. "C'mon in," he said, waving them into the two chairs that filled up the rest of the room. The window was open and the smell of cat came in on the breeze. It didn't seem to bother Tom, who was chewing with gusto.

"We're disturbing your lunch," Matt said.

"I don't mind," Tom said, taking another bite. "Sorry I can't offer you any."

Matt laughed. "We're going to the cafeteria."

Tom made a face. "Good luck. Don't order the chipped beef."

"Don't worry." Matt turned to Lisa. "You wouldn't think a man so brave with the big cats would be such a coward in the cafeteria."

Tom smiled a broken-toothed smile at Lisa then looked back at Matt. "So to what do I owe the honor?" He took another bite, which seemed to finish it.

"I wondered if you knew what happened to the cages the jags were delivered in."

"The cages?" Tom scratched his head. "No, I never saw them."

"Do you know if they belonged to Jacky?"

"I think so. Why? Are they missing?"

"Not missing. As far as I know. I'd just like to look at them."

"Well." Tom got up and opened the door. "They could be down in storage."

Matt nodded. "I haven't checked there yet."

Back in the exhibit area, Koo was heading for the service door.

108

Tom stopped him. "Do you remember those cages the jags arrived in?"

Lisa watched Koo's face become blank. His light blue eyes seemed almost transparent. An expression of polite interest appeared like a mask. "Cages?"

"Yeah. About a week ago." Tom turned to Matt. "When was it the jags arrived?"

Matt thought. "A Tuesday. Week ago last Tuesday." He too seemed to have noticed Koo's face. He asked him carefully, "Do you remember?"

"I remember. I was here late that night because Raji had a bad cough and I was waiting to see if I should call Doc Landry. Mrs. Winston came in all excited. She told me the jags' quarantine was over and they'd be arriving within the hour."

"And they did?"

"They arrived before nine."

"How'd you get them into the exhibit cage?"

"The two truckers and I did it. It wasn't hard."

Lisa had the feeling that he was leaving out important information. But since she had no evidence to support her feelings, she said nothing.

"When did you leave the zoo that night?" Matt asked.

"Like I said, I was watching Raji. I spent the night on the couch in the office."

Tom added, "Koo or I have occasionally stayed on the couch when we're worried about one of our cats."

Matt nodded. "I want to see the cages. What did she do with them?"

Again, Lisa felt a change in Koo, a sudden attentiveness, although she couldn't tell if she was just imagining it.

"Nothing that night. The next day she brought her van up to the service door and asked me to load them."

"And you did?"

"Yeah."

"Then what?"

Koo shrugged. "I don't know."

"And that's the last you saw of the cages?"

Koo nodded.

"Did you notice anything unusual about them?"

"Like . . . what?"

"Anything. Anything at all."

Koo shook his head.

"Okay. Thanks. If you remember anything, will you let me know?"

"Sure," Koo said and walked away.

The three of them stood watching Koo walk toward the service door. He moved like a dancer, lithe and silent. He had slim hips and legs, and his jeans fit as though they had been painted onto him.

Matt turned to Tom. "Did you see the cages Wednesday morning?"

Tom shook his head. "I was off that Wednesday. What is it you want to know about those cages?"

"I don't know. Maybe nothing. But one thing I do know. They were too heavy for her to handle by herself, even empty. Whether she brought them to storage or to her ranch, someone must've helped her unload them."

"Someone must've helped her do what?" a voice behind them asked.

Lisa turned and saw John Winston standing in the open doorway with a young man who, Lisa guessed, must be his son Johnny. When no one answered Winston, he repeated, "Helped her do what?"

"Unload the cages," Matt said.

"What cages?" Winston asked, while Johnny stared in the

direction of the jaguars' cage with unfocused eyes as if he were under sedation.

"The cages the jaguars arrived in. We think they belonged to Mrs. Winston. I'd like to know where they are now."

"May I ask why?"

"Just a hunch I'm following. Do you know what she did with them?"

"I've no idea."

Johnny had walked over to the jaguars' cage and was staring at one of the animals that was now lying on the shelf.

"Do you know if she took the cages to her ranch?" Matt persisted.

"Jacky didn't discuss the ranch with me. I haven't even been up there in years." He paused and looked at Matt without friendship. "I should think that as the director of a zoo from which funds have been stolen, you'd be more concerned right now with the fact that Alden Vining took over fifty thousand dollars from right under your nose than with some cages, wherever they may be."

"Of course I'm concerned about the theft. But there's nothing I can do about that now."

Lisa felt herself breathe in. Matt was leaving himself wide open. She wasn't surprised when Winston said, "There was a great deal you could have done about preventing it from happening—if you'd known what you were doing."

Matt said nothing. His face reddened.

Satisfied, Winston went on, "There's a special board meeting tonight to look into the theft. I'd like you there, with a list of all requisitions you've approved in the past five months and notes on why you approved them."

Matt's face was the color of a sunset now. "That'll take me all day," he managed. "I've got duties, things I—"

"And don't you think I've got obligations as well?" Winston cut in. "I don't enjoy the thought of spending the rest of my day going through Alden Vining's books, but that's just what I'll be doing. This affair is damn inconvenient. Especially when we're trying to get the bond issue." He headed for the door, then turned and said, "Come, Johnny."

"I'm going to stay here for a while," Johnny said in a flat voice without looking at his father.

Winston left without another word.

Tom O'Rourke shook his head. He seemed embarrassed at having witnessed the scene. "Well, to work," he muttered and returned to his office.

Johnny stood with his back to them, bent over in front of the jaguars' cage. His shoulders were shaking.

Matt and Lisa exchanged a look. Then Matt went over to Johnny. He stood behind him for a moment, not daring to touch him. Finally, he said softly, "Is there anything I can do?"

Johnny shook his head.

Matt pulled a handkerchief from his pocket and handed it to Johnny. He blew his nose. "Funny how the jags get to me," he said. "They meant so much to her. If you knew me at all, you'd know how ridiculous this is, me crying."

"I don't think it's ridiculous to cry."

Johnny cleared his throat. "I always knew she cared, that she'd be there for me. No matter what."

Matt nodded.

"You know, she never hurt anybody. She didn't like hurting any person, any animal, anybody. And this is what it got her."

He met Matt's eye, then walked out of the building. The door banged behind him.

"Sad," Lisa said, touched by the depth of his grief.

Both jaguars were pacing again. The futility of their circular movement made Lisa feel even sadder.

112

"Poor unhappy guy," Matt said. They were silent, watching the cats. Then Matt looked at his watch. "Let's go check out the storage barn and have lunch. Then I better get busy on those requisitions or I'll be here all night."

"That's not really necessary, what he asked you to do, is it?"

"I don't think so. But he seems to."

They left the Big Cats House, joined in sadness.

18

THE STORAGE AREA was a wooden garagelike structure in back of the Elephant House. Their footsteps echoed on the concrete floor as they entered. They passed several power lawn mowers, some rakes and flower pots stacked near the door and walked down a central corridor past rows of fencing, storm windows, plumbing fixtures, and folding chairs.

"Everything including the kitchen sink," Lisa commented as they passed a pile of stainless steel sinks.

"It's all here," Matt agreed. "New and old alike. Supposedly, Charlie Avery knows where everything is down to the last fence post. I haven't ventured into his territory much."

"Hello." The voice was high-pitched and came from somewhere near the ceiling. A small man, as lithe as a spider monkey, scrambled down a ladder, a box of light bulbs under his arm.

Matt introduced Charlie Avery to Lisa, then asked about the cages.

Charlie didn't even have to think about it. "She brought a cage over a week ago last Wednesday, late afternoon. I helped her get it out of her van."

"Only one?"

"That's right."

"One of ours?"

"No. Her own, but she asked me to store it here for her."
Charlie was already walking rapidly toward the back of the
building. Matt and Lisa followed. Cages of varying sizes were
piled high against the wall next to the open rear door. Charlie
pointed toward a cage on the floor in the corner. It looked
like a large wire mesh box with a metal top and bottom.

Lisa went over to it and opened the door, which was slightly
ajar. The cage smelled of disinfectant. The floor was of a
corrugated material that looked like rubber.

"She left it out back," Charlie was saying. He waved with
his free hand toward the ceiling-hung garage door. "Asked
us to clean it and store it for her until she needed it."

Lisa walked around the cage. She read, "The Winston
Ranch" embossed on its metal top. "Did you notice anything
unusual about the cage?" she asked.

"Unusual?"

"Anything out of the ordinary."

Charlie shook his head. "Nope. But I didn't look for anything either."

"Could you describe the condition of the cage?" Matt asked.
"For example, how dirty was it?"

"Well, she said the cat had traveled in it—for days, I guess.
It warn't no rose garden." He laughed. "But we hosed it out
and cleaned it with this all-purpose disinfectant we use." He
opened the cage door wide. "See, the floor is constructed out
of plastic. You slide it out to clean it, then push it in and it
locks in place." He demonstrated, sliding the floor section
out from the frame, then snapping it back.

Lisa looked closely at the sliding floor and then looked at
Matt to see if he had noticed what she had—there was a
space of about two inches between the floor and the metal

bottom of the cage. Matt had noticed. He slid the floor all the way out of the cage. There was nothing in the space at the bottom.

"How about under here?" Matt asked. "Find anything?"

Charlie shook his head and laughed again. "Nothing you'd care to know about."

Matt slid the floor back and snapped it in place.

"Are you sure it was a week ago last Wednesday she brought the cage over?" Lisa asked.

"Yeah, positive. Late Wednesday—around five thirty or six. I remember because I was pissed off at Tom O'Rourke's heap of a car. I was trying to get the carburetor adjusted so she'd quit stalling on me."

"What's that about Tom's car?" Matt asked.

"Oh, see I lent him my pick-up so's he could go deer hunting down the Cape with some buddies. I took his old Ford."

"When did you make this exchange?"

"Tuesday after work. He drove over to my house, left his heap, took my truck. Wednesday morning his car made it to work all right, in through the service gate and right out back here. But after work I couldn't get it started. He'd told me he sometimes had trouble with the carburetor, so I figured that was it."

"Did you get it started?"

"Finally. After we unloaded the cage. Mrs. Winston waited to make sure. Said she'd give me a ride if I couldn't." He shook his head. "Nice lady."

Matt and Lisa nodded.

"What should I do with it?"

Matt looked at the cage. "Just keep it here for the time being. Thanks, Charlie. We'll find our way out."

Lisa watched Matt wolf down his hamburger in the zoo cafeteria. "You in that much of a hurry?" she asked.

Matt put the almost finished sandwich back on the plate. "Sorry. I have to confess, John upset me. I'm afraid he's after my scalp and I'm anxious to get all that information he wants. I think I better make a good impression tonight."

Lisa speared a limp lettuce leaf and watched him take another bite. "You've made a good impression on me."

He smiled.

"I can't imagine anyone taking his work more seriously, caring about the animals and people under his supervision more than you do."

He sipped his coffee. "You're maybe a little prejudiced in my favor."

"I think any of those board members who can't tell the kind of person you are is just plain stupid."

He put his hand over hers. Then he pushed his chair back. "Ready?"

"Sure." She wondered if the chipped beef could possibly be worse than the soggy salad. She hoped she'd never have the chance to find out.

"Why did Jacky bring only one cage to storage?" Lisa asked as they walked back to the administration building. "And why didn't she bring it the night it arrived? Why the next night?"

"When I offered to ask Charlie to get the cages the night they arrived, she refused."

"Okay, then, the next morning. Why didn't she bring it over Wednesday morning? Why Wednesday late afternoon and why only one?"

Matt nodded, perplexed also.

"And another thing. Tom O'Rourke took that Wednesday off. Right?"

"Apparently he went hunting on the Cape. You think that's significant?"

117

"I don't know. Maybe, maybe not. We better get up to the ranch, take a look around."

"Can you do it tomorrow?"

Lisa thought for a moment. She'd been spending a lot of time and energy on the problems at the zoo and not enough on her work. Harry Travera had thought the zoo series was a good idea, but had warned her that her piece on the East Braeton incinerator dispute had to be in Wednesday after the selectmen's meeting, and it better be good. "It's not the feature fluff, it's the local issues that are our meat and potatas," he'd said with his Boston accent. "Tomorrow," she promised Matt.

"Good. I'll do my rounds first. Can you meet me in the parking lot at nine?"

Lisa agreed. She walked him to his office door and said, "Good luck at the board meeting tonight."

As she headed down the corridor toward the front door, she heard the muffled sound of an argument coming from behind a door. JOHN WINSTON, JR., PUBLIC RELATIONS was lettered in black on frosted glass. She heard a loud voice, unmistakably John Winston's, ". . . get you to a bloody psychiatrist and fast." The voice was enraged beyond discretion.

The other voice, too low to hear, was overridden.

"You bet it is—a degenerative disorder. I blame him. I'll see that he's fired, out of here—then you'll get help."

Lisa hardly dared to breathe.

"If Koo goes, I go. I love him," Johnny's voice said.

"You never used to . . ."

"You're wrong. I always . . ."

Heavy steps toward the door and John's voice loud with frustration, "I won't listen to this. You're a sick boy. Sick and I'll . . ."

Lisa ran on tiptoes past Johnny's door, down the corridor, and out the front door. In front of the building she almost bumped into Addie Whitney returning from lunch.

118

"Hi, Lisa, have a nice lunch?" Addie smiled.

"Uh huh," Lisa replied. She thought of the work Addie and Matt would have this afternoon getting the information that John Winston had demanded. Addie wouldn't be smiling for long.

—— *19* ——

THEY HAD BEEN DRIVING for about an hour. Comfortable, Lisa sat back and allowed memories to engulf her. She turned to Matt. "Remember when you took me to my high school dance and all the girls nearly died of envy."

"Yeah—remember we danced cheek to cheek and pretended we were madly in love."

"Hah. What do you mean pretended?"

Matt glanced at her, laughing, then turned his eyes back to the road.

"Couldn't you tell I had this incredible crush on you?"

"But you were only . . ."

"Fourteen. Old enough." Her feelings that night came back to her now, as strong as the sunlight that was heating up the inside of the car.

"I never knew you felt that way about me."

"Course you did," she insisted. "You used to have that look on your face then, the one you have right now. Everytime I mooned over you. Mostly embarrassed. Maybe a little pleased. Very protective."

He looked at her and smiled. She could see it all coming back to him. "Yeah. I guess I did know how you felt. And

120

I liked it. But I was ashamed that I liked it. You were just a kid, for God's sake, and I was supposedly grown up, but I was so shy and bumbling I could hardly talk to a girl my own age. God, you don't know how badly I wanted to."

She did. She'd known so much about him. She'd felt sorry for him then, just as she had when she saw the way he looked at Jacky Winston at the Gala. In fact, she realized now, his shyness with girls his own age had given her hope as a child that maybe he'd wait for her to grow up. "I did know."

He glanced at her again. "You were a smart kid. A very special kid."

"Tell me about you and Jacky."

He began eagerly, as if he'd been waiting for her to ask, as if he'd been waiting to talk about it. "I met her in zoology lab. I knew right away—the way she looked, the way she handled her scalpel, that sureness of hers. And then when I got to know her better, everything about her was what I wanted."

"Everything?"

"Everything. There were a few things that bothered me. But even those things attracted me . . ."

"Like?"

"Like her energy. She couldn't sit still. Even when she studied, she'd pace with her book in her hand. She had to be on the move, always looking for a 'kick,' as she put it."

"A kick? Like drugs?"

Matt shook his head. "Not that kind of kick. Oh, she smoked a little pot, like everyone then, but nothing crazy. No. She wanted excitement, and the incredible thing—to me—was we found our excitement in the same place."

"Exotic animals."

He nodded. "She wanted to learn everything about them. She wanted to photograph them, care for them. Unlike me,

121

she wanted to hunt them, to capture. Not kill, of course. And never anything illegal. She was into conservation long before the Endangered Species Act."

"So why did her energy bother you, especially since a lot of it was directed toward animals?"

He slapped his hands against the wheel. "Because she was too much for me and I knew it. I knew it from the first moment she smiled at me in that special way she had. I knew that she'd tire of me."

Self-fulfilling prophecy, Lisa thought. But she said, "Maybe she was the kind of woman who would always tire, could never be satisfied."

He was quiet for several moments, then asked, "Did I ever tell you what a kind person you are?"

"Yes. About twenty-five years ago. Right after you moved in when I carried Bagels in after he'd been clobbered by a hit-and-run." As she said it, she experienced the delicious feeling of connectedness that the memory made her feel toward Matt. They had a history together and they'd loved each other—in their own way.

"Well, I was right about you. And you're right about Jacky. In a sense, anyway. She did tire of people. It was more like she'd use them up and then go on to the next. And then there was her fascination with money and power. That was always there. When she met John Winston, she saw everything she'd always thought she wanted."

⸻

At first sight the Winston Ranch seemed to be only a collection of modest white clapboard farm buildings. There was a high fence around the property. Matt pushed the buzzer beside the gate before he noticed that the gate was unlocked.

"That's funny. That gate is always kept locked."

He opened the gate, drove in, and shut it behind him. "It's

122

important to keep the gate locked. There's the danger of animals getting loose or vandals getting inside."

As they drove along the road, there was no sign of life except for what sounded to Lisa like a cow mooing. "What's that noise?"

"Sounds like old Sadie, Tony's milk cow."

"Tony?"

"Jacky's caretaker. I wonder if he's been told."

"Noisy, isn't she?"

"Too noisy." Matt looked worried.

They bumped along the rutted road past a cottage toward a barn, unpainted and tilted like a house of cards about to go down.

Matt stopped in front, jumped out, and ran inside. Lisa, following more slowly, noticed piles of old boards and debris next to the door. The smell of hay and cow dung was heavy as she followed Matt into the dimness of the barn.

As she stepped over the threshold onto the wooden floor scattered with hay, she breathed in the sweet-sour odor and then held her breath as Matt shouted, "Don't come in."

At the sound of his voice, the cow's bellowing, which had stopped when he entered the barn, started up again, drowning out whatever else Matt might be saying. Whatever it was, Lisa was not about to obey. She walked carefully toward the cow's sound as her eyes grew accustomed to the dimness.

The man was sprawled in a stall face down in the hay, and even from where she was standing, about twenty feet away, Lisa could see that the back of his head had been blown away. She looked away, then back again. Matt was kneeling beside the body. A black and white cow nuzzled his arm, but he didn't seem to notice. A stool was turned over behind the body, as if the dead man had been sitting there when he was hit and had fallen forward. A milk pail lay overturned beside him.

123

Matt stood up and walked clumsily toward Lisa. He took her arm and together they went outside. Standing in front of the barn he gulped air while the cow started up her wailing again.

"Who?" she asked while he tried to steady himself.

"Tony."

"Oh, no."

"He's been dead for hours."

They walked the short distance to the farmhouse. The door was unlocked. Matt entered first, Lisa following.

They walked quickly through the house. Their footsteps echoed on the wooden floors. "Looks as if nothing's been touched," Matt said.

They went into the kitchen in the back of the house. The kitchen was neat with a brick floor and cheerful red-checked curtains at the windows. Matt went to the telephone on the counter. He looked in a small leather book he took out of his jacket pocket and dialed a number.

Lisa filled the kettle on the stove and found a jar of instant coffee on the counter.

"Cohen's direct line," Matt explained. "Ah, it's ringing." His face relaxed somewhat. "Lieutenant Cohen? Matt Yates. I'm calling from Jacky Winston's ranch in Crossbourne, New Hampshire. It's the caretaker. Tony Farina. He's been shot." He paused. "There's no doubt about that. He's dead, all right." Another long pause. "Right." He hung up.

Lisa handed him a cup of coffee. "Drink this. You're white."

Matt took a few sips. Then he said, "Cohen's coming. He's taking the police helicopter to the Crossbourne police barracks."

"How long will it take?"

"Maybe an hour. He's calling the local police. They should be here soon."

Together they walked through the house again, checking

it carefully. All tidy and in order. Tony's bedroom behind the kitchen. Upstairs one large bedroom with a pale yellow silk comforter and a large old-fashioned bathroom with thick yellow towels. Lisa didn't have to be told it was Jacky's room. There were two other bedrooms and another bathroom upstairs.

"I better milk poor Sadie before she bursts," Matt said. "Come on."

Walking back to the barn, she remembered. "The cage."

"Forgot all about it."

"Me too."

She waited, sitting on the edge of the stall, turned away from the sight of the body while Matt milked Sadie. Then together they began their exploration of the barn. The section of the barn they were in was sealed off from the rest by a sheet of plastic.

Lisa found a doorlike flap and they stepped through the plastic curtain onto a new wooden floor. This larger section of the barn was under construction. Lisa smelled fresh lumber and plaster. They stepped over sawhorses and workers' tools. Lisa walked to a corner where there was a pile of odds and ends, copper pipes covered with a tarpaulin, and some window frames in the process of repair. "Matt," she called. "Here."

The cage was there, a duplicate of the one she'd seen at the zoo, on the floor next to a power saw. A trickle of white powder marked its vinyl flooring.

"We better not touch it until Cohen arrives," Lisa said as Matt leaned closer.

They went back outside and sat in the sun. Although the sun was strong, Lisa couldn't stop shivering.

The local police arrived, two eager young sergeants whose names, Field and Ross, fit their bland young faces perfectly. One asked many questions that seemed irrelevant to Lisa while the other painstakingly wrote their answers into a notebook.

Lisa was relieved when Cohen and Hughes drove up with another man, who carried a large black bag.

Cohen noticed her before he even greeted the others. He squinted into the sun and said, "I know you from somewhere."

Hughes prompted him. "Lisa Davis. The case at Addison University last year."

"Of course." Cohen put out his hand and said in his bantering way, "Lisa. How nice. What the hell are you doing here?"

"Hello, Irving," she replied, shaking his hand. It was too good to be true. She'd stayed up nights plotting how she would handle him if they ever met again. She had resented his treating her with condescension during the investigation of the deaths at Addison. Her resentment seemed to have focused on his calling her by her first name. She'd made it her business to find out his.

If he was taken aback, he didn't show it. Only Officer Hughes reacted. He laughed and glanced at her with appreciation. A small victory, indeed, she thought as Cohen was led into the barn by Field and Ross.

They gathered around the body—Cohen, Hughes, and the man with the black bag.

Matt and Lisa stood outside the group waiting for Cohen to finish so they could show him the cage. Sadie stood in a nearby stall watching them with anxious brown eyes. If only she could talk, Lisa thought.

When Cohen had finished his investigation of the body, he and Hughes followed Lisa and Matt to the section of the barn under construction. As they stepped onto the new wooden floor, Lisa felt a chill go through her that had nothing to do with the plastic-covered windows and open sections of roof.

126

"What are they constructing here?" Cohen asked.

"I'm not sure," Matt said. "This may have been the new animal nursery. Jacky told me she'd begun work on it, but she didn't tell me it was to be in the barn."

Lisa wondered if the nursery would be completed now. Probably not. Who would want it now that Jacky was dead?

They circled the cage. Cohen touched the white powder on the cage floor with his fingertip. He brought his finger to his nose and sniffed. "Did you touch anything?" he asked.

Matt and Lisa assured him they hadn't.

"Is it cocaine?" Lisa asked.

"Very likely." Cohen sent Hughes to get Peter, the man with the bag. Peter dusted for prints on the cage and collected samples of the white powder as Cohen and Hughes continued to examine the area.

Lisa sat on a pile of metal heating ducts propped against the wall and watched them.

When they'd finished with the cage, Cohen began his questioning while Hughes took notes. "Now, how did you happen to be here today, Mr. Yates?" Hmm, Lisa thought, Mr. Yates. Had she cured him of condescension? Or would Matt have rated a Mr. anyway?

As Matt told Cohen his suspicions about the cages, Hughes's hand raced across the page.

Cohen looked surprised. "I find it hard to understand why you didn't tell me about the cages when you first sensed something wrong."

"Because . . . because." Matt struggled for words. "It seemed stupid. It was just a wild guess."

"Not so wild, it would seem. Why don't you let me be the one to judge whether an idea is stupid or not."

Matt nodded.

"Is there anything else you'd like to let me in on?" Cohen asked.

"I can't think of anything."

"Then tell me about Tony Farina."

"He'd worked for Jacky for years. He had no family. This was his home. And he was killed right before he milked Sadie last night."

"Milked who?"

"The cow."

"What cow?"

"I milked her and moved her to another stall. It was her mooing that brought us into the barn in the first place. She hadn't been milked last night and the milking stool was tipped over right behind Tony's body."

Cohen looked exasperated and Lisa was sure he was going to scold Matt about touching evidence before the police arrived, but he only sighed and rolled his eyes up to the rafters. "Why don't you start right at the beginning," he said, "from the moment you turned into the driveway, and tell me everything, every impression you had and everything you saw, including Sadie and any other cows you happen not to have mentioned."

As Matt talked, Lisa glanced at Hughes, who was smiling as he wrote, the perfect audience, the perfect sidekick. She looked away when he noticed her watching him. She disliked ingratiating people. They always made her want to be nasty.

Cohen turned to her. "Ms. Davis," he said, coming down hard on the "Ms.", "would you please tell us your impressions and, if I may ask, how you happen to be here."

Lisa told him of her old friendship with Matt and of her assignment to the zoo as part of her duties as reporter for the *Times*. As for impressions, she had nothing to add to Matt's recital. "You really think that was cocaine in the cage?" she asked.

"Seems to be. We'll do a lab analysis for positive identification. You knew her well, Mr. Yates. Do you think she'd

128

smuggle cocaine into the country with those jaguars?"

"I wouldn't have thought so. She was a principled person. I don't know how desperate she was."

"What do you mean 'desperate'?"

"I mean desperate for money so she could leave her husband."

Cohen nodded. "Can you think of any reason why someone would want to kill Tony Farina?"

"None that I know of, except maybe Tony saw the person who helped Jacky bring the cage here."

"So you think someone helped her with the cage?"

"It's likely. And we've been wondering why she brought only one of the cages here. Why not the other one as well?"

"Well, you told me that the other cage, in the storage building of the zoo, didn't appear to have traces of the white powder. Maybe they had cocaine only in this cage."

Matt nodded. "Could be."

"What makes you think someone came with her when she brought the cage here?"

"Because Tony couldn't have helped her unload it. He had a bad back and couldn't do any lifting."

"What about the men working here?"

Matt shrugged. "I don't know about them. Maybe she couldn't count on their being here. They're not here today. I don't actually know that she had someone with her. It's possible that she came alone."

"I'll look into that." Cohen stood up. "Are you going back to Braeton now?"

"As soon as I make arrangements for someone to come in and take care of the animals. They haven't been fed since yesterday. I'll have to make sure they are before we leave."

"Please stop at the station when you get back," Cohen said as they left the barn.

As Lisa and Matt walked back to the farmhouse, the ambulance was pulling up in front of the barn. Back at the house Lisa washed the coffee cups while Matt made phone calls. Why am I doing this? she asked herself. Trained to be a cleaner-upper at mother's knee. Good girls leave clean sinks. Old values die hard.

When she finished, she sat with elbows on the kitchen table wondering about Jacky Winston's values. A lover of animals and nature willing to sell a dangerous drug like cocaine? Well, whoever said human beings were consistent, consistently good or bad?

Matt put down the phone. "That's a relief. Adam Klinger, son of a local farmer. He's helped Tony often. He'll feed them and will stay as long as needed. Come on, I'll show you the ranch before we go."

Outside the ambulance was heading out the gate. Cohen and the others stood in front of the barn. Matt drove along a narrow road bordered by high wire-mesh fences. In the enclosures Lisa saw elephants and bears and many kinds of hoofed animals. Matt stopped the car and pointed to the top of a hill where a lithe spotted cat with a small head stood watching them.

"Her pride and joy. A female cheetah."

"Like the one I saw at the zoo yesterday."

"Right."

As he spoke, the cheetah bounded away. "She's beautiful," Lisa said.

"They're the fastest animals in the world at short distances."

Lisa watched until the animal disappeared into the bushes. She felt a surge of anger that such a beautiful animal should be penned up. "Wouldn't she be better off in Africa running free?"

"They're an endangered species now. Their best chance at survival is breeding in captivity."

130

Later as they drove past New Hampshire woods on their way home Lisa said, "So you think the killer could be the person who helped her bring the cage to the ranch. Maybe he killed her, then killed Tony so he couldn't identify him."

Matt nodded.

"Couldn't be Alden," Lisa continued. "He was arrested."

"He's out on bail. He was at the zoo yesterday afternoon cleaning out his desk."

Lisa was thoughtful. "But he loved her. He stole the money because he loved her."

"You are a romantic."

"Well, it's true, isn't it?"

"I don't really know Alden. He's a careful man. I'd never have thought him capable of theft." He paused. "Or of love."

Lisa looked over at him. Was he jealous of the man Jacky had loved, even now that she was dead?"

"What about John Winston? He could've killed her, then Tony. He was in love with someone else, wasn't he?"

"He's been in love with some someone else for years. But Jacky was a great asset to him—at the zoo, in the community. They were the perfect couple. He wanted it to stay that way and he had nothing to lose, financially, that is."

"I've got a question for you," Lisa said. "Why was Tony murdered last night? Jacky died over a week ago."

"You think that's important?"

"It could be."

They were silent for a while, then Matt said, "I keep thinking of Koo. The night the jags arrived, I had the feeling that Koo was helping her even though he stayed in the background. He said he was spending the night there."

"Why?"

"Because Raji, the male tiger, had a cough."

"Did he really have a cough?"

"Yes. But I'm not sure it was bad enough to warrant Koo's staying. Maybe there was more to it."

"Like watching the cages—the cage with the cocaine in it, I mean."

"Could be."

"So maybe when you saw Jacky and Koo, they hadn't even had a chance to take the cocaine out of the cage. They'd just emptied the jags into the big cage and then you came along."

"Jacky got me out of there in a hurry," Matt said thoughtfully. "That left Koo."

"Do you know that Johnny and Koo are lovers?" Lisa asked, suddenly remembering what she had heard.

"I've heard gossip. But how do you know that?"

"Yesterday, after I left you, as I was walking by Johnny's office, I heard his father shouting at him. He said Johnny had a 'degenerative disorder.' He said he'd kick Koo out. And Johnny said he loved Koo and that if Koo went, he'd go too."

Matt shook his head. "Poor Johnny, and he's still reeling from losing Jacky. You'd think John would know to lay off for a while."

Lisa looked at him. She liked his serious eyes and the sensitive set of his lower lip. She thought of how her ex-boyfriend, Brad, would have responded to hearing about Johnny's love for Koo with some macho joke about fags. She leaned over and kissed Matt's cheek.

He touched his cheek with a finger. "What's that for?"

"For being you."

He laughed. "With all that's been going on lately, I wish I were somebody else."

"Well, don't."

He looked at her. "Okay," he said, then after a while, "Thanks."

132

20

It was the middle of the afternoon when Matt and Lisa drove up in front of Braeton Police Headquarters.

"Go right in. Lieutenant Cohen's expecting you," the deskman said.

Lisa opened Cohen's office door. Winston and Johnny were sitting across the desk from Cohen. Hughes sat near the window, pen in hand as usual.

Cohen half rose. "Come in. Come in," he said, genial as a party host. "Hughes. Chairs."

Hughes left the room and returned with two folding chairs. Winston and Johnny scraped their chairs closer together.

Winston's face was grim. "Tony was such a decent guy. Why in God's name did they have to kill him?"

"We don't know," Cohen answered equably. "He wasn't robbed. His wallet with sixty bucks was in his pants pocket."

"Did they steal anything else?"

"Well, since we don't know what was there, we don't know yet if anything was stolen. But nothing seemed to be disturbed."

"The animals were all right, as far as I could tell," Matt said.

Winston put his head in his hands.

"I expect you'll want to go up there yourself and check out the property," Cohen said.

"I called Adam Klinger," Matt told Winston. "He's worked for Tony and he said he'd take over until he hears from you."

"What were you doing up at Jacky's ranch, anyway?" Winston asked with suspicion.

"We were looking for one of the cages I asked you about yesterday. Remember? The cages the jags were transported in."

"Oh, the cages," Winston said, sad and preoccupied. "And did you find them?"

"We did."

"Where?"

"Charlie had one, and the other was in the barn. In back."

"So what does that tell you?" Winston asked impatiently, "other than that Jacky owned that cage and brought it back to her ranch?"

"Well, I don't think she brought it by herself. It was too heavy for her to manage, and Tony couldn't lift anything because of his back."

"Maybe you're making too much of it." Winston shrugged. "She dumped the cage in the unfinished section of the barn. So what does it matter if someone helped her with it or not?"

"Yeah. Why does it matter?" Johnny asked, his voice high and thin.

"It could matter," Cohen said, easily entering the discussion. "You see, we found something in that cage, something that shouldn't have been there."

"What?" Winston asked, his forehead creased with concern.

"Cocaine. We stopped at the lab on the way back, just to be sure."

Lisa was watching Johnny's face. She saw the color drain out of it.

134

Winston's angry explosion hurt her ears. "Ridiculous!" he shouted. "What would Jacky be doing with cocaine?"

Cohen said nothing.

Still angry, Winston asked, "You think this person who helped her bring the cage to the ranch had something to do with the cocaine and with the deaths—hers and Tony's?"

"It's possible. We're looking into a number of possibilities. We'll know more when we get lab reports. I hope we'll have some answers for you soon."

Winston nodded.

Cohen stood up. "Well, that's all for now. We'll be in touch."

Outside Lisa climbed into the station wagon beside Matt. She watched Winston and Johnny drive off in a sleek black car.

Hughes shut the door behind the group and sat down in the chair opposite Cohen.

Cohen leaned back in his chair and put his feet up on the desk. "So what do you think, Tim?" His eyes were closed.

Hughes sat forward, pleased to be asked his opinion. "What I think is that she got ahold of the coke in Brazil and taped a package of it under the flooring before she put the cat in." He looked over to Cohen for a response, but Cohen was still lying back in his chair, eyes closed.

"See, that way no one would've gone near that cage until the dangerous animal was out of it. So she got through Customs—no problem. Then, when Mr. Yates showed an interest in the cages the night they arrived, she got him out of there fast. Moved the cage with the cocaine to her ranch, then removed the cocaine and sold it."

"Hmm," Cohen said, eyes still closed. He liked working this way. Knowing that Hughes would bring up all the ob-

135

vious points, he could listen while another part of his mind searched for connections that were, perhaps, not so obvious.

"And then something happened between her and her accomplice," Hughes was saying.

"Accomplice?" Cohen asked innocently.

"The one who helped her bring the cage to her ranch. He must've been in on the deal. Then it went sour. He knocked her on the head, dumped her in the bear's den."

Suddenly Hughes jumped out of his chair and bent over Cohen's desk. "Hey," he shouted, causing Cohen's eyes to fly open, "y'know, Tony Farina could've been involved in the drug deal too. The accomplice—we'll call him Mr. X— could've gotten greedy, wanted it all for himself, killed both Mrs. Winston and Tony so's he could pocket all the profit."

Cohen leaned forward, allowing the chair to pull him up slowly to a sitting position. "You're forgetting a couple of things," he said with a smile.

"What?"

"Well . . ." Cohen looked at Hughes's disappointed but eager face. "There's the time span, first of all. Jacky Winston was killed a week ago Sunday night or early Monday morning. Tony Farina was killed over a week later. Why the week in between?"

Hughes frowned. "Well, I don't know, but there could be a perfectly good explanation . . ." He trailed off, unable to come up with one at the moment.

"And," Cohen continued good-naturedly, "there is the puzzling question of the differing styles of murder."

"Styles?"

"Yes, indeed." Cohen was enjoying Hughes's confusion, as he always did. "In Jacky Winston's case, the murderer did everything he could to make us think her death was an accident, a drunken fall into the bear pit. Even the broken heel turned up right next to the fence where it could have landed

136

if it had broken off while she was on top of the fence."

Hughes nodded.

"Whereas Tony Farina's death was clearly premeditated murder, with no attempt to disguise the fact."

Again Hughes said, "There could be an explanation. Like maybe the killer didn't have time to plan Tony's murder."

"Could be. But we want to be aware of any pattern or any change in a pattern. We want to keep our eyes open for anything unusual."

Hughes nodded, his eyes open wide.

"Now." Cohen rubbed his hands together. "Alibis. Let's check them for the two murders, shall we?"

Hughes began to flip pages in his notebook, and Cohen leaned back in his chair again. The telephone buzzed. Hughes picked it up. "Lieutenant Cohen's office." He listened for a few moments, then said, "Yes. We'll want the All Points Bulletin sent out immediately with a description of Vining and his automobile." He hung up and said, "Vining is gone. Our boys tried his home and office. His car's missing, but he doesn't seem to have packed any clothes or other belongings."

Cohen sighed, but continued, "Okay, alibis. We might as well start with him. Vining."

Hughes shuffled the pages, then read, "Claimed he'd been at home sick in bed the night of the zoo Gala. He said Jacky Winston had telephoned him at about two A.M. very upset. She said she had to talk to him, that she'd be at his place in half an hour. She never showed. He had no one to back up his story, saw no one, talked to no one that night except for that telephone call from Mrs. Winston.

"As for yesterday afternoon, when Tony Farina was murdered, Vining was out on bail, as you know. He went to the zoo to clear out his desk. We have no information on him for the time between five and six when Tony Farina was murdered, but seeing as how he's disappeared this way, I think that could be an indication of guilt."

Hughes closed his notebook on his finger and looked hopefully at Cohen. Cohen's eyes were closed again. For a moment Hughes thought Cohen had spoken, but then he realized that his boss was only humming to himself. "Shall I go on?" he asked.

"Of course."

Hughes flipped pages. "Here we are. John Winston. He said he left the Gala at about midnight the night his wife was murdered and was home in bed by about twelve thirty. The housekeeper, Janine Lund, corroborates his story. She was in her room watching an old movie on TV when she heard him come in. He was alone. She asked about Mrs. Winston, and he said that he'd been tired and left early without her. She asked him if he wanted some hot milk, but he refused, saying he was going up to bed. She went to bed herself soon after and slept until morning.

"As for yesterday, Winston claims that he spent several hours going over Vining's books in the treasurer's office before Vining came in, then went to the cemetery, stayed there for a while at his wife's grave. On his way home, he stopped at a fast-food place—Ho-Ho's—on Route 63 for supper. It was the housekeeper's day off. Ho-Ho's was crowded. He didn't think anyone would remember him. Then he went home and changed his clothes and went to the board meeting.

"We also heard some stories about the Winstons' marriage. From the Clayburghs and Mr. Yates as well as Mrs. Lund the housekeeper. Mr. Winston admitted that he had lovers, but claimed that he and Mrs. Winston were good friends, worked well together. No one challenged that. But Yates and the Clayburghs did say they seemed to be arguing the night of her death."

Cohen summed up, "So, neither Vining nor Winston has an alibi for either occasion."

"Right. Neither do Johnny Winston, Koo, or Matt Yates."

"Then there's the question of the heel," Cohen said from his reclining position. "I'm pretty certain the heel was placed in the leaves early that morning by someone who was waiting for the chance. But who could have done it? Why? And how did that person get into the zoo without entering at the main gate?"

"The killer must've put it there," Hughes said eagerly, "so we'd think she fell into the den by accident. And the only person who passed the gate guard that morning was Koo. Could be we got an open and shut case."

"An open and shut case on an open and shut gate," Cohen mused, tenting his fingers as he lay back in his chair. "There is another way into the zoo."

"But it means going through the tiger enclosure," Hughes reminded Cohen. "And besides, if Mr. Yates told us the truth, the locks to those gates were changed when he took over, and the only key is in his safe."

"You think Mr. Yates might not be telling the truth?"

"You told me, 'Never take the truth for granted,' " Hughes quoted.

Cohen sat up. "I did, didn't I? You're catching on well, very well."

Hughes blushed with pleasure. "And there is always the possibility the heel was there all along and the boys missed it in all those leaves."

"Yes," Cohen said, but he looked as if he was thinking of something else.

21

THAT EVENING Lisa was working at her kitchen table. She'd finished her first article in the zoo series and was adding the details of last night's protest march on Braeton Town Hall to her incinerator story, when the telephone rang.

It was Matt. "I'd like to talk to you." Under his casual voice she detected the snap of tension.

"Where are you?"

"In my office."

It was after eight. Lisa had already eaten dinner. "I'll bet you've been there since you left the police station. I'll bet you haven't even had dinner."

"Anna's genes, I see."

She laughed. "I'm afraid I didn't make pot roast and chicken soup today. How about grilled cheese?"

"I'll be there in half an hour."

When he arrived, she put his sandwich in the toaster oven and poured two mugs of tea, which she set down on the coffee table.

Matt sat on the sofa and warmed his hands on his mug. "Can I help?"

"It's all done." A good smell of melting cheese and toast filled the room.

She brought his sandwich in and watched while he bit into it. She remembered how Addie had watched him with such adoration as he chewed his croissant the morning he discovered Jacky's body. It occurred to her that he was the kind of man a woman would always want to mother. Was there any long-range satisfaction in that? Depends. On what else there was. She found herself wondering, again, why he had never married. Because he'd always been in love with Jacky, as he said? Or was he just a loner, like the cheetahs he'd pointed out to her?

"I couldn't work," he said. "I kept seeing Tony lying there."

"I know." She herself had been tormented by the image of the dead man all day.

He picked up his tea and allowed the steam to bathe his face. Then he put the mug back on the table. "What I've been thinking about is that . . ." he hesitated, then said, "that I caused his death."

"What do you mean, caused his death?"

"Well, we think and the police seem to think Tony might have been murdered by a person who was involved with Jacky in a scheme to smuggle cocaine into the country in the jaguar's cage."

Lisa nodded.

"So Tony could've been killed because he was involved in the deal."

"Right."

"But," Matt continued, "the other possibility, as you and I discussed today, is that Tony was not involved in the drug deal, but was murdered because he knew the identity of Jacky's murderer. Don't you see, if it hadn't been for me, no one would have given those cages a thought. I was the only one who linked the cages with Jacky's death.

"And yesterday I went around the zoo asking about them, looking for them, alerting Jacky's murderer to the possibility

141

that the police might follow the trail of the cage to Jacky's ranch, to Tony, who knew the murderer's identity because he had been at the ranch when Jacky and her accomplice brought the cage there.

"If it hadn't been for me, Cohen would never have known about those cages and it would never have occurred to him to check with Tony at the ranch."

Lisa thought about it as Matt sipped his tea and watched her. Finally, she said, "No. It's not because of your talking about the cages that Tony got killed. If the murderer was worried about Tony identifying him, he wouldn't rest easy just because the police didn't go right up to the ranch and question Tony. He'd be worried that at some point they would or that Tony would talk to someone—you or Winston or someone else—and mention the person who helped Jacky bring the cage to the ranch, and then suspicion would be raised."

"You really think so?"

"I do. Because if Tony saw the killer, then the killer had to silence him." But even as she reassured Matt, a doubt began to gnaw at her. Something she'd forgotten about? Something important? She couldn't think what it was.

Matt looked relieved, however. He picked up his plate and took another bite of his sandwich. "I feel much better," he said. Lisa felt worse. She made more tea and hid behind a cheerful face.

"Would you like to read my first feature article on the zoo?" Lisa asked when they'd finished their tea.

"Sure."

She handed him the typed sheets and watched him as he read.

When he looked up, he said, "It's all about me."

"It's about Jacky too. And the breeding program and the

new jags. I'd like to talk to some of your department heads and other keepers."

"Why don't you meet me at the zoo at eight tomorrow morning," Matt suggested. "We'll do my morning tour a little earlier than usual. Then I'll have time to introduce you to some staff members you haven't met."

After he left, Lisa got into bed. But she couldn't sleep. Matt's concern had started her thinking. She knew she was missing something. But what?

22

LIEUTENANT COHEN whistled as he entered his office Wednesday morning. It was seven forty. He'd just come from a fight with Eva who was complaining about his hours. Was he so eager for work as a way to escape her nagging? He took off his jacket and hung it on a wire hanger on the coat rack in the corner. The telephone on his desk rang. He picked it up. "Cohen," he barked.

"Listen carefully," a muffled voice said. "The person known to you as Koo, Eustis Cooney, served time for selling drugs in St. Crail, Arkansas."

Cohen had grabbed a pencil and was writing it down. "Wait a minute. Tell me that again slowly."

"So you can trace the call? Sorry. Eustis Cooney. St. Crail, Arkansas." Click.

"Jesus," Cohen said. "What the hell is this?" He ripped the sheet from the pad and clicked the phone.

Hughes, walking into the office just then, was surprised to hear his boss say, "Yes, FBI, and fast."

Several minutes later the two policemen were driving toward Koo's rooming house in the poorer section of Braeton. "It was an unidentified caller, disguising his or her voice. The information he gave me was correct, though. It checked out with the feds. Eustis Cooney served time in Arkansas for selling cocaine."

"Is he wanted?"

"Naw. Clean as far as they're concerned. We'll pick him up for a little chat."

The address—137 Ward Street—turned out to be a sagging gray frame house. The suspicious woman who answered their ring told them that Koo had left for his job at the zoo over an hour ago.

"May we use your phone?" Cohen asked.

She made them show their IDs again before she reluctantly let them into the house.

The telephone was a pay phone in the linoleumed hallway. At Matt Yates's apartment there was no answer. Cohen had better luck with John Winston. "I need to get into the zoo," Cohen said. "Can you meet me there right away?"

"Of course. I just have to get dressed. Twenty minutes all right?"

"Thanks. That'll be fine." Cohen and Hughes went back to the car while the landlady stood in the doorway watching them.

"He won't be there to let us in for about twenty minutes. We have time to stop and pick up some coffee and doughnuts on the way," Cohen said.

"Hey, now you're talking," Hughes said, cheered. A late sleeper, he never had time for breakfast before he came in in the morning.

Lisa drove into the zoo parking lot a little before eight. It was a clear cold morning. She heard an unearthly sound coming from the zoo. She knew it was only the roar of a lion, but it made her flesh creep.

She sat in her car until Matt drove up, feeling that uneasy

145

sensation she'd had last night, wondering what it meant. She reviewed all that had happened yesterday. She was missing something, she thought, but didn't know what. She tried to remember everything that had occurred at the ranch. She was sure there had been some clue she'd overlooked. But she couldn't think of it now.

She thought about how Matt had tried to shield her from the sight of Tony Farina's body. Matt was a considerate man. He seemed much the same as when she'd known him so many years ago. She remembered her initial reaction of disappointment when she first saw him again a couple of weeks ago. Now she realized that the disappointment was changing into something else—something comfortable, but not exciting. Definitely not exciting, although at first she'd hoped. . . . Now she thought she understood how Jacky must have felt about him.

When he pulled up beside her, she walked over to greet him. He got out of his car, long legs first, then reached back in for his briefcase. They entered at the gate with Matt's card. "I'll just go into my office and see if there are any messages. Want to come with me?"

The bright crisp morning beckoned to Lisa. "I'll go on ahead."

"Okay. Meet you at the Elephant House. Ten minutes."

"I'll say good morning to Solomon. See how his tooth is today."

Lisa walked along the path beside the tiger enclosure. It seemed to her that the tigers and zoogoers were separated from one another only by the low wire-mesh fence. But as she got closer, she realized that the fence was there to restrain the observers, not the tigers. A deep moat kept the tigers inside the enclosure. The fence kept the humans, not as naturally wary as tigers, from wandering in and possibly falling into the moat.

146

Lisa stepped off the path onto the grass and went up to the fence to get a better look. Not a tiger in sight. She stood still for a moment as she heard again that deep roar that made her skin turn to goose bumps. The padlocked gate in the fence near her led to a gravel road inside the enclosure that turned into an embankment and crossed the moat. On the enclosure side of the moat the road was barred by another gate the width of the embankment. If a tiger tried to cross the moat by way of the road, it could get only as far as the first gate and, therefore, could never get nose to nose with a curious tiger-watcher at the fence gate.

Matt had told her that service vehicles used this entrance for clean-up and landscaping every few weeks. On the far side of the enclosure, the side that bordered the highway, there was no moat. Instead there was the double fencing that Matt had told her the Braeton Board of Selectmen had insisted on for public safety when the enclosures were built several years ago. There were gates in these two fences also so that vehicles could enter the enclosures directly from the highway. But, as Matt had explained, security was enforced by the heavy-duty locks for which the only key was securely tucked away in his office safe.

Standing at the gate, Lisa was suddenly aware of an odor that she couldn't quite place. The enclosure was well cared for, a grassy field, mown but not manicured, with several outcroppings of ledge and a number of trees. The place was hardly odor-free, she thought, as a breeze brought the sharp sour odor of cat. But it wasn't the cat smell that puzzled her, it was another smell that had a cutting edge to it. She sniffed again. The smell seemed to be coming from the gate, sharp enough to make her eyes sting.

The roaring split the air again, and Lisa turned away from the gate. She walked toward the sound, feeling that shiver of fear that was almost like pleasure. The sound

147

drew her to the old stucco building that was the Big Cats House.

Heart pounding, she stood in the doorway and looked in. The lion was standing in his cage, half-crouched, with his head thrust forward. As Lisa watched, he roared so loudly that the building seemed to shake. She stepped back.

"Hello," said a quiet voice behind her. She whirled around, the human voice seemed as inappropriate to her as if the lion had spoken.

Koo stood on the path behind her. He wore overalls and high rubber boots and carried a coiled hose. His bright yellow hair fell over one eye.

Lisa caught her breath. "Why does he do that?"

"Do what?"

"Roar like that?"

Koo smiled and she could tell he was pleased by her fear. "Letting the world know he's here, that he's king of all he surveys. C'mon in, he won't eat you."

But Lisa didn't want to go in. She didn't know why she was so frightened, but somehow the combination of Koo with his strange smile and the big cats was too much for her.

"No. I'm meeting Mr. Yates," she said, backing off.

There was something really weird about Koo, she thought as she continued on to the Elephant House. It's as if he were on stage, always trying to make some kind of impression. That smile—so calculated to put people off balance somehow.

In the Elephant House she watched the animals methodically lifting hay with their trunks and pushing it into their mouths. Only Solomon stood still, his large head hanging, his trunk limp.

Soon Matt came up beside her. "Solomon, here old boy," he called. He held out a piece of apple.

The elephant slowly lifted his head, then let it sink.

148

Matt looked worried.

Solomon lifted his head again and was looking at Matt.

"Here, boy. Here," Matt called. Solomon moved slowly toward him, his trunk swaying from side to side. When the elephant got to the fence, Matt reached over and patted his head. Solomon held his head at a funny angle and turned only his good side toward Matt. He didn't take the fruit Matt held out to him.

In the Big Cats House Koo methodically went about his morning chores. He got the mop and bucket from the service room. Raji wasn't in his cage. Koo couldn't tell whether he was in his sleeping quarters or outside in the enclosure. He pressed the control on the wall outside the cage. The metal grating between the cage and the sleeping quarters slid down and locked closed with a click. Koo unlocked the door and entered the empty cage. He placed his cleaning equipment inside and then locked the door behind him with one of the keys on the chain attached to his belt. The zoo security rules dictated that all cage doors be locked at all times, even when the cage was empty or you were inside it working. Koo thought the rule was stupid, but he knew that if Tom or Mr. Yates came along and he hadn't followed it to the letter they'd can him.

It's pretty dumb, though, Koo thought. If you just close the door behind you, the animals aren't going to figure out how to open it. He laughed to himself at the idea that lions and tigers were plotting their escape, that they would rush to a door that was closed and turn the handle with their paws.

He tried to cheer himself up by imagining Raji balanced on his hind legs turning the catch with a forepaw. But the absurd idea didn't lift his spirits. He was too burdened with problems. Jacky Winston and now Tony Farina. The burden of responsibility was more than he could stand. But what could he do about it?

He peered into the sleeping den through the locked grill. Raji met his eye, rising from the hay with a low growl, like a saw biting into fresh wood. Not friendly this morning. Probably a little hungry, but feeding time wasn't until late afternoon because, if they were fed early in the day, the animals would sleep the day away instead of being frisky and interesting for the visitors.

If only work would dull this ache in his heart. He turned the hose on the tiled walls of the cage. Caesar roared again and the sound seemed to start Raji growling. Koo smiled as he hosed down the cage. There was something about the big cats that moved him deeply. Their power. Their mystery. They seemed to understand much more than man gave them credit for. He liked the way they carried themselves with dignity and grace. He admired their assured sexuality. They mated when they wished, with whom they wished. Man's moral standards had nothing to do with them.

Koo finished with the hose and unlocked the cage door, stepped out and locked it again behind him. He coiled the hose and placed it on the floor. Then he returned to the service room and filled the pail with hot water and disinfectant. He carried the mop and pail back to the cage door, unlocked it, stepped inside, and locked it behind him.

It always gave him a strange feeling to be locked into any of the big cats' cages—as if he had voluntarily given up his humanity, as if he could become a beast. Raji was snarling and hurling himself against the door. He probably thinks I'm putting meat in the feeding tray, Koo thought and then smiled at himself because of his habit of wanting to know what his cats were thinking and feeling. What he really believed was that Raji, who seemed like one of the most intel-

150

ligent of the cats, was frustrated because he had been robbed of his freedom and that restraint of any kind kindled his fury at humankind.

Koo poured some of the solution from the pail onto the floor and set to work with the mop. He whirled around suddenly as he heard the sound of the barred door to the tigers' sleeping quarters opening, the grate of metal against metal. As he turned, he saw Raji squeezing under the opening door, like an alley cat squeezing in at the bottom of a slightly open window. Koo gasped as the tiger sprang. His hand went to his overall pocket for the bottle of ammonia he kept there for emergencies, but his hand was knocked away. The mop went flying out of his grasp and he felt the pail of hot detergent solution spilling over his legs as he was thrown to the ground by the weight of Raji's body. But how could the door to the sleeping den have gotten unlocked? he thought as he felt the tiger's hot breath on his face, and his consciousness was shattered by the searing pain of claws and teeth.

Solomon was rubbing the right side of his huge face against Matt's arm with affection. The left side of his face, which he kept averted, was swollen. "Who will examine his jaw—the vet?" Lisa asked.

"Al Kramer's going to examine him. He's a regular people dentist, but he's had some experience with exotic animals."

"But Solomon's so big. Won't it be dangerous?" She watched the powerful beast rubbing himself against Matt's shoulder. It made her nervous to know that the elephant could hurt Matt seriously if he wanted to. But Matt seemed unworried by Solomon's strength. He petted the animal's face, taking care not to venture near the sore part of the jaw.

"We'll try a local anesthetic. We don't want to use a general unless we have to. It's difficult to determine just how much to use with such a large animal. And a mistake in dosage could lead to serious consequences."

Suddenly Solomon quivered under Matt's hand and his ears flapped wide like the sails of boats running before the wind.

Then Lisa and Matt heard it too. Screams, coming from the direction of the Big Cats House. Matt moved fast. Ducking under the rail, he was at the door of the Elephant House in a moment.

Solomon stepped back, lifted his trunk and trumpeted. Perhaps he was insulted at being abandoned so suddenly. More likely he, too, was responding to the screams that were now louder and more agonized, Lisa thought, as she ran after Matt. She entered the Big Cats House right behind him.

Koo lay on the floor of Raji's cage. He was pushing against the chest of the tiger with a torn and bleeding arm. Raji tore at Koo's body, attacking again and again with his teeth, holding him down with his claws. Koo's screams filled the room.

Matt rushed to the cage and grabbed the broom propped up against the wall. He pushed the broom handle through the bars of the cage and poked the tiger in the head. Raji snarled with rage and turned toward the broom, letting go of Koo, who slumped to the floor and lay still. Jumping at the broom handle, he tried to grasp it with his paws, to get his teeth into it.

Matt jiggled it and moved it rapidly from side to side, luring the animal away from the inert body on the floor. The tiger chased and batted the broom handle, with fast-moving paws. Matt pushed the broom through the bars and then threw it in an arc toward the far side of the cage. Raji jumped and pounced on it.

Matt reached into his pocket, took out a dart gun and shot at the animal's left flank. The dart hit. Lisa, motionless with horror, saw it sink into the tiger's flank until only its red flag protruded. The tawny fur of the tiger's hip twitched.

Raji worried the broom for a few moments longer. Then, as if suddenly remembering the much more interesting prey he had left, he lifted his large striped head and snarled again deep in his throat. Lisa's breath caught as she watched him start to turn back toward Koo. But suddenly the tiger's head dropped, his legs seemed to collapse under him, and he fell heavily on top of the broom.

Matt opened the cage door with his key and closed it behind him. Lisa felt terror as Matt's foot grazed the belly of the unconscious tiger, but Matt didn't even seem to notice. He bent down and gently lifted Koo. Half-carrying and half-dragging him, he eased him to the cage door.

Lisa held the door open as Matt lifted Koo under the armpits and pulled him through the door, the heels of his boots bumping along on the tiled floor of the cage.

Lisa couldn't take her eyes off the tiger, lying where he had fallen, a trickle of blood coming from his parted lips, his paws, stretched out before him, stained red.

23

As soon as Koo's feet cleared the door, Lisa slammed it shut and turned the key in the lock. As she bent down to help Matt, Lieutenant Cohen and Officer Hughes appeared in the doorway.

Matt was working over Koo, pressing his arm above the place where blood was spurting from a deep wound.

In a moment, Cohen was at his side. "Get the kit," he said to Hughes. Cohen tore off a strip of Koo's mangled shirt and tied it above the arm wound. Matt began to cut away the torn rubber overall and shirt.

Hughes raced back into the room with a large black box from which he unrolled bandages. He and Cohen pressed them against Koo's wounds. As they cut away more of the shredded shirt, Lisa saw the wounds on his chest, great ugly gashes from which blood poured. His neck and chest were a mass of blood, the rest of his skin the color of paper.

Lisa felt light-headed, her face as cold as if she also had lost too much blood. The sour cat smell filled her nose and mouth. Air, she thought. And fast. But her legs started to buckle. She made it to the doorway and took a couple of steps outside. She felt herself sliding to the ground and the spinning in her head began to change into a soothing blackness.

Someone was lifting her. A hand around her waist. Another protecting her neck while her head wobbled like a rag doll's.

"Easy now. Easy," said a voice that sounded familiar. Whose voice? She tried to open her eyes. The smell was strong. The smell prickled her nose. She fought to get away from it. With great effort she tried to open her eyes. The hand holding her neck rested on the side of her face. It was his hand that smelled bad. The smell made her cough. She jerked her head away and opened her eyes. Johnny Winston was holding her like a dance partner. He had just asked her something.

"What?" she asked, her face close to his.

"You all right now?"

"What happened?" But even before she got the words out, she remembered. They were standing on the path in front of the Big Cats House.

"I caught you just as you were falling," Johnny said, still holding her. "I was coming up the path and I saw you."

"Nice catch, son," John Winston said, as if Johnny had just caught a forward pass. He stood beside his son. "Are you sick?" he asked Lisa. Then he looked over her head and into the Big Cats House. "Oh, my God," he said.

The three men were still working over Koo. Only moments had passed since Lisa had begun to feel faint. John Winston hurried into the building. Johnny followed. Lisa, still weak, trailed behind them.

Cohen was getting stiffly to his feet, his big face creased and unhappy. Matt, still squatting beside Koo, looked up at Lisa and shook his head.

Johnny Winston bent over his lover. He took his face in his hands and a tear splashed onto the still cheek. Then another. Lisa looked away.

Matt came over to Lisa. His hands were covered with blood. Blood stained the front of his shirt. "You all right?"

155

She nodded. She swallowed.

Johnny was sobbing. He held Koo in his arms, rocking him.

They all watched.

Finally, John Winston touched Johnny's shoulder. "Come on, son. Come on." Lisa had never heard him speak with such gentleness.

Johnny lowered Koo's head to the ground and allowed himself to be led away.

They stood just outside the building as Hughes radioed for an ambulance from the police car.

Winston held Johnny, who sobbed against him.

"How did it happen?" Cohen asked Matt.

"I don't know. We were in the Elephant House, Lisa and I, when we heard his screams. He was in the cage with the tiger. He'd already been badly mauled. I managed to divert the tiger with the broom and then anesthetize him so I could go in and get Koo out." He paused. "It was too late."

"Why would he have gone in there with the tiger?" Cohen asked.

"He wouldn't. He knew better. We all knew Raji could be dangerous. Koo wouldn't have gone into the cage if the tiger was there."

"Well—how did it happen, then?" Cohen persisted.

"He was washing down the cage. Raji would've been locked out of it, either in his sleeping den or in the outdoor enclosure beyond. Somehow the door between the cage and den must've gotten unlocked."

"How?"

Matt shrugged, puzzled. "The control box is on the wall outside the cage door. You need a key to use it."

"And who has the key?"

"The keeper, Tom O'Rourke, Koo and I."

"That's it?"

"There's an extra key locked in the keeper's office. In back." Matt pointed toward the office.

Cohen nodded to Matt. "Show Officer Hughes."

Hughes and Matt went back into the building.

Cohen turned his attention to John Winston and Johnny, who still stood with his face pressed to his father's shoulder although he was no longer sobbing.

Winston held his arm protectively around his son.

"I'm sorry that I must interrogate you at such a difficult time," Cohen said.

"Go ahead," Winston replied. "Then I'll take Johnny home."

"When I called you this morning at a little before eight, you told me you could meet me at the zoo in about twenty minutes to let us through the gate. And you did. In fact, you were right on time. You let us in with your gate card, but then you said you had to drive over to your son's apartment and pick him up. Do you usually come in together, you and your son?"

"No. But Johnny called right after I spoke to you this morning and asked if I could pick him up because his car is on the blink. I told him I could, but that first I had to meet you here and let you in, as you seemed to be in a hurry to get into the zoo."

"I see," Cohen said.

Matt and Officer Hughes were walking back toward the group. Hughes carried a plastic envelope with a bunch of keys in it. Cohen nodded at Hughes, who put the envelope in his pocket and took out his notebook and pen.

Johnny lifted his face from his father's jacket. Winston handed him a folded hankerchief and he wiped his eyes.

"What time was it that you called your father to ask for a ride?" Cohen asked him.

"I think it was just after eight." Johnny's voice was husky. He cleared his throat.

"How did you know your car wasn't operable?"

Johnny cleared his throat again. "I knew it last night and called the tow truck. They're towing it to the garage later this morning."

Cohen nodded. Hughes was writing it all down. Lisa wondered where it was leading.

"Why didn't you call your father last night to ask for a ride?"

"I don't know."

"How would you have gotten here if your father hadn't picked you up?"

"I could've taken a cab."

"Did you consider walking over to the zoo?"

There was a pause. "I didn't think about it. No."

"Why not?"

"I don't know. Question of time. I've got a lot to do today."

Cohen nodded, but wasn't ready to drop it yet. "If you walked from your place, how long would it take?"

Johnny shrugged. "I've never actually . . ."

"But if you did?" Cohen pressed.

"Maybe twenty minutes. I don't know."

"Thank you. You two may go. I'll talk to you later if I need any more information."

Winston and his son turned and walked down the path, Johnny leaning into his father. Winston had his arm around Johnny.

Lisa looked at the two policemen. Hughes was still writing. Cohen was examining the cage door. The tiger stirred. Lisa heard a siren.

"I'll go open the gate for the ambulance," Matt said. "I don't think the entrance guard is on duty yet. It's not quite nine."

"Oh, right," Cohen said. He seemed deep in thought, watching the tiger as he stretched his paws, began to lick at the blood.

"All right if I go too?" Lisa asked.

"Fine. Fine," Cohen said distractedly.

"What a tragedy," Matt said as they walked toward the gate.

"Could it have been an accident?"

"I don't see how."

Lisa shivered.

Matt sighed. "Another lost day. Poor Koo. What an ending."

"I've got to attend that incinerator meeting at Braeton Town Hall this afternoon at four, and my story's got to be in this afternoon. But I think we need to discuss Koo and the rest. Could you meet me for dinner?"

"Sure."

"That Italian place on Main?"

"Six thirty okay?"

"Good. My treat. It's my turn. I can't swing Mon Reve, but Rico's is perfect."

Lisa slipped out to the parking lot as Matt opened the service gate with his card. When she looked back, he was climbing into the ambulance next to the driver. She watched the ambulance start up the hill.

Walking to her car, she shivered as she wondered what it would feel like to be torn apart by a tiger. Would the pain be unbearable? Or would you be rendered unconscious immediately? Such thoughts put all one's little problems into perspective.

24

MATT WAS DEPRESSED during dinner. "I almost called you and canceled," he told Lisa. "I'm not fit company." He refilled their glasses with the jewel-red wine and drank.

"Did you have to close the zoo today?"

"No. They moved the body out. Then business as usual. It's getting . . ." he paused, "almost routine."

"Does Cohen have any idea how it happened?"

"If he does, he's not confiding in me." Matt drank more wine. "But he did tell me that the reason he was at the zoo early this morning was because he learned from an anonymous caller that Koo served time for drug-dealing. He wanted to talk to him."

"That's interesting."

The waiter arrived with their veal parmigiana and spaghetti.

"I had to mention Koo in my story on Jacky's death," Lisa said. "By the time it's printed it'll be old news."

Matt waved a hand, his cheeks flushed. "Don't worry. It's already old news. The *Globe* and the *Herald* scooped you. They hung around the zoo all afternoon."

Lisa sighed and wondered if her ex-boyfriend Brad Newman had been the one assigned to the story. She was glad she hadn't been there.

"I'm sorry you didn't get your tour today."

"We'll try again when things calm down," Lisa said.

Matt seemed distracted.

They ate.

"Good," she said.

"Mm." He was looking out the window over her head.

"So, Cohen didn't ask you anything else?"

"No. Not really."

"And you don't think they've got anyone in mind?"

Matt shrugged. "Us, maybe. You and I were the only ones in the zoo, other than Koo, when it happened. Cohen checked the gate records—in and out."

"Isn't there any other way in?"

Matt shook his head. "No usable way."

"Are you finished?" the waitress asked Matt. She was very young and her face looked fresh and scrubbed.

Matt pushed away his plate.

She took their plates.

"You didn't eat a thing," Lisa said.

"Can't stop thinking of Koo—and the others."

"You think Koo's death was an accident?"

"I don't know what to think. Cohen sent in some lock experts. They've taken apart the locks and doors to see how the mechanism could've failed." He turned his wineglass slowly at the stem. "I guess it could happen." He didn't sound convinced.

"Could it be he left it open, didn't know Raji was there?"

"We've very strict rules against leaving sleeping den doors open while working in cages."

"So maybe he didn't follow the rules."

"Maybe."

"Maybe he was thinking of something else and forgot to lock it."

"Maybe. But that kind of 'forgetting' just doesn't go with zoo work."

The waitress was standing before them. "Coffee?"

Matt looked inquiringly at Lisa.

"No," she said. "Let's go."

Outside in front of her car Lisa wanted to continue their discussion. She hoped that if only she could sort out some of the facts, the murders and the theft might add up to some identifiable pattern. "How about stopping for a drink?" she asked.

"I'm really tired. It's been one hell of a day. But why don't you come over to my place. I'll give you a little brandy, then I'm sending you home."

He gave her directions. His apartment was not far. They each drove in their separate cars.

The apartment was big and comfortable, the second floor of one of Braeton's old Victorian houses. Lisa threw her jacket on the chair in the hall and entered a high-ceilinged living room with polished dark floors and a marble fireplace framed in dark wood. Matt's furniture was old and comfortable.

Matt bent over the fireplace and lit the fire, which was already laid. Then he poured brandy into large snifters.

"It's charming, really a lovely room," Lisa said, watching spears of flame leap upward.

"Thanks. Just a little brandy for you," he said in his big-brother voice, handing her the glass. "You've got a long drive home."

Lisa smiled. "That's nice. I like being taken care of."

"You don't mind if I stretch out, do you?" Matt lowered himself into an arm chair and put his legs up on the ottoman.

Lisa sat on the old flowered sofa next to him.

162

He sipped and put his glass on the floor. Then he leaned back with his arms behind his head and sighed.

Lisa sat forward in her chair. "So, it could have been an accident."

Matt closed his eyes. "An accident," he repeated. "Probably."

"But if it weren't, how does Koo's death fit in with everything that's happened?"

Matt gave a bitter laugh. "When I'm feeling paranoid, I think that the way it fits in is that someone's out to get me, take the directorship away from me."

"Like who? Who would want to do that?"

Matt sighed. "Oh, I don't really mean it. But you know, the theft, Jacky's murder, Tony's murder, Koo's accident—if that's what it was—are not only tragedies in themselves, they are harmful to the zoo and to me because I'm responsible for everything that happens at the zoo."

Lisa was silent, thinking about the theft and how it might relate to the murders. "The theft alerted us to the fact that Jacky needed money—or thought she did—in order to leave her husband."

"But we don't know if Jacky's need for money actually had anything to do with her death."

"We don't know. Yet. But it's possible that Jacky was involved in some kind of money-making scheme, probably cocaine smuggling, that led to her death. And to Tony's death, if he, too, was involved or if he could identify the person who was, the person who helped Jacky bring that cage with the cocaine up to her ranch."

"And the person who helped Jacky was probably Koo," Matt added. "And we know Koo served time in Arkansas for dealing. So Koo could've been the mastermind of the cocaine scheme, the person Tony could have identified."

"And then Koo's conveniently mauled to death by a tiger," Lisa said. "I wonder."

The fire was down to red glowing embers. Lisa got up and pushed the charcoaled pieces of wood together. A spurt of flame shot up between them and with it an image flashed in Lisa's mind of the cage she had seen in the unfinished section of the barn at Jacky Winston's ranch. Suddenly she knew what had been bothering her ever since she saw it— the cage had been clean except for the traces of cocaine on the floor and in the trough under the flooring. The cage stored at the zoo had been clean also. But Charlie had told them that it had been his job to clean it, that he had hosed it down, even scrubbed it out. "You wouldn't want to know," he'd said of the condition of the cage when he'd received it.

The cage left at the ranch must have needed cleaning also after the jaguar had been transported in it. And since it had been cleaned, why were there still traces of cocaine left? Why hadn't they been hosed away? Could it be that someone had placed those traces of cocaine in the cage after it had been cleaned? That there had been no packet of cocaine taped under the floor of the cage?

"Matt," Lisa said urgently. "Matt, the cocaine could've been planted in the cage. So that the police would . . ." She stopped in mid-sentence. She was quiet, remembering. "So that we would discover it," she amended.

Matt shifted in his seat and made a snoring noise, then was still. His chest moved rhythmically. His face, soft in sleep, looked like that of a child.

"Matt," she said, wanting him awake, desperate for his opinion, and then she fell silent as she remembered something else. Watching the rise and fall of his chest, hearing the hiss of his deep breathing, she remembered what he had said last night. She remembered his fear that he had, by searching for the cages at the zoo yesterday, caused Tony's death. She remembered and she breathed in sharply as the facts she knew shifted into a new pattern in her mind.

Somehow, what seemed to her like the most important fact of all was a smell. She knew what that smell was now, and she thought she knew what it meant. But to make sure, she'd have to take some chances. It meant getting into the zoo now. Right now. The evidence—if there was evidence —might be there now. By tomorrow it might be gone.

Should I wake Matt up and ask him to go with me, she asked herself?

She bent over him and put her hand on his shoulder. She looked at his face, childlike in sleep. She knew what he'd say without even asking. He'd tell her to wait until tomorrow, to leave it to Cohen. She thought she knew him well enough now. He didn't take chances. He didn't follow his instincts. A good man, a quiet plodding man. He'd say no.

Already he was stirring, uncomfortable in his chair. He wouldn't sleep long. In a little while he'd wake up enough to realize he wanted to be in bed. So, if she really wanted to go to the zoo, she had to decide quickly before he awoke.

Still she hesitated. She was afraid. She pictured what it would be like at the zoo now—dark, scary, the lion roaring in the night. But is it really dangerous? She checked her watch. Eleven twenty. No one would be there. Not at this hour. If there were any cars in the lot, she wouldn't go in. If the lot was empty, she'd park and be in and out in a matter of minutes. If she found what she was looking for, okay. If not, she'd just get out.

No. It wasn't really dangerous. And, if worse came to worst, and someone came by, she'd just say she'd left her article in Matt's office and he'd given her the gate card and key to come pick it up.

Still, she hesitated. I'll leave him a note, she decided. Then, if I don't come back before he wakes up, he'll know where I am. She found a piece of paper, wrote the note, and propped it against the hibiscus plant on the coffee table.

She tiptoed over to his chair and knelt in front of him. Gently she slipped her hand into his pants pocket and took out his wallet. She took out his zoo gate card. Then she reached into his pocket again and found the ring of zoo keys. They jingled. Matt shifted in his seat and groaned. Lisa stayed still until he settled down again. Then she slid the wallet back into his pocket and walked quietly out of the room. She picked up her jacket from the hall chair and let herself out of the apartment.

25

NIGHTTIME BRAETON was peaceful. A few couples from the university were walking arm in arm as Lisa drove by. Some muffled music escaped from the disco at the Braeton Arms.

She tried to piece together what she knew. Matt had gotten a hunch that the cages held a secret and that the secret related to Jacky's death. He had asked around the zoo to find out where the cages were and found one of them in the storage barn. Then, the next day, yesterday, she and Matt had driven to the ranch to look for the other cage. They had found Tony murdered and they had found the cage they'd been looking for with traces of cocaine in it.

Lisa was now on the highway. As she passed the fences that contained the lion and tiger enclosures, she had another thought. Whoever placed the cocaine in the cages and killed Tony had also called Lieutenant Cohen with the tip about Koo's drug involvement. And he must have murdered Koo too. But why? Why murder Koo? Why not just set up the evidence against him and let justice take its course?

She turned into the zoo parking lot, empty and still, lighted only by a big October moon. Koo's murderer had gotten into the zoo even though his entrance was not recorded on the gate record. And Lisa thought she knew how he had done it.

She closed the car door softly even though there was no one around to hear it. She let herself in at the gate with Matt's card. Once inside the zoo, she smelled the animal smells, rich and deep, earthy odors she was getting used to. She heard animal noises on the night wind—high-pitched calls of birds or monkeys and the deeper voices of larger animals. A roar that seemed to originate in her own stomach shook her and she felt a surge of excitement in her chest. She was close and she knew it.

She tried a few of the keys before she found the one that let her into the administration building. Inside the halls were dark. She didn't want to chance putting on a light, so she rummaged around in her pocketbook and found her small flashlight. She followed its beam down the corridor until she came to Johnny Winston's door. On Matt's key ring she found the master key and used it as she had seen Matt do. The door swung open into the dark office, lighted in bands by moonlight coming in through the venetian blinds.

She took deep breaths. The room seemed to be pressing in on her with its secrets. Her hand holding the flashlight was shaking. The flashlight beam found a door in the back of the room. She opened it. A closet. A jeans jacket hung on a hanger. Beside it hung an empty suit hanger. Some cardboard boxes were piled on the floor. She reached over and uncovered one of them. Braeton Zoo stationery with Public Relations, John Winston, Jr. across the top in gold embossed letters. She closed the closet door, went to the desk, and began to go through drawers. The top drawer was filled with the stationery she'd seen in the closet. The other drawers contained papers, manila folders, pens, paper clips, and other office odds and ends.

She pulled open the deep right-hand lower drawer. It was

designed to be a file drawer, with metal tracks on the sides. But Johnny Winston had not used it for that purpose. No, he had not used it for that purpose at all. Before she actually saw what she was looking for, Lisa knew it was there. She smelled it—the odor that had been teasing her memory ever since Johnny had picked her up when she fainted in front of the Big Cats House this morning. She opened the drawer wide and there it was. She took a handkerchief out of her pocketbook and used it to lift out the small plastic bottle. The bottle had a squirter top. It was partially filled, and she had no doubt about what was in it. Her nose told her loud and clear. Ammonia. She wrapped it carefully in the handkerchief and slipped it into her jacket pocket. Then she looked back into the drawer and saw the pair of old worn jeans. She pushed them aside and saw the heavy workboots encrusted with dirt. Picking up one of the boots, she touched the dirt with her fingertip. Damp. Can the police test the soil on this boot and tell where it came from? she wondered. Probably.

She sat there for a moment, thinking of the implications of what she had discovered and felt a prickling of tension in the back of her neck and down her arms. The key, she thought. He had to have it to get in through the gates to the enclosure. He wouldn't have dared carry it with him. What if Lieutenant Cohen had said, "Let's take a look at your keys"? What if he had made him turn out his pockets? No. After he used it, he would have left it here with the clothes, to be safe. She took everything out of the drawer and lifted the drawer out. Then she ran her hand along all the surfaces of the drawer. She checked the other drawers and under the desk top. No key. She checked the closet again. Nothing.

Matt felt himself falling. He'd been balanced on his toes at the top of the fence enclosing Anuk's den. Now he was toppling headfirst into the open jaws of the bear. His scream woke him. He sat bolt upright in his chair. His neck was stiff, his arm asleep where he'd been lying on it. The room was dark. Embers glowed in the fireplace.

"Lisa," he said, then more loudly, "Lisa."

Then he saw the note propped up on the coffee table. He read it, then dug into his pockets. His keys and card were gone. He jumped up and ran into the bedroom where he kept an extra card and set of keys in his bureau.

Lisa sat in the desk chair and thought hard. Johnny had killed Koo. He must have slipped into the zoo through the gates of the tiger enclosure just before she and Matt arrived this morning. She could pinpoint the time because of the strong smell of ammonia she'd noticed at the gate when she stopped on her way to the Elephant House. He let himself in through the gates at the highway, and he squirted himself with ammonia to keep away any tigers that might be roaming the enclosure.

He must have ascertained that Raji was inside in his sleeping quarters, then sneaked into the Big Cats House and gotten the key that unlocked the sleeping den from Tom O'Rourke's office. He must have unlocked the door between the cage and the sleeping quarters while Koo was working in the tigers' cage. He would have known that Raji would be hungry and that there would be no way for Koo to save himself. He would have counted on Matt's regular morning zoo tour starting a half an hour later, as it usually did, not knowing that Matt and Lisa were meeting early this morning.

Then, after killing Koo, he must have hidden his muddied shoes and clothes in the drawer and dressed in clean clothes he kept in his office. He must have called his father, who had just received the call from Cohen, and arranged to meet him at the gate and pretend that they had driven to work together.

But where was the key? Either he had hidden it well or he had taken it with him, Lisa thought as she began to search the file cabinet under the window.

Why would Johnny kill Koo? Had their love gone sour? Was Koo threatening Johnny in some way? Why would that love suddenly turn to hate? A possible answer came to her, though she couldn't trust it yet. Could Johnny have killed Koo because he believed Koo killed Jacky? The evidence pointed to Koo as Jacky's murderer. Maybe Johnny believed Koo did it. Maybe that's why. But Johnny didn't kill Jacky, Lisa thought. I'm sure he didn't.

Lisa sat up. Suddenly she knew what she had not known until this very moment. There were two killers. There must be two. Because she could not believe that Johnny had killed Jacky. Stop being so sure, she cautioned herself. Just because you don't think Johnny killed Jacky doesn't rule it out as a possibility. All right, all right, she answered herself. Possibilities. We are dealing with possibilities. Possibility number one: there are two killers, one who murdered Jacky and Tony. And a second killer, Johnny, who killed Koo because he believed Koo had killed his stepmother.

And the first killer . . . Lisa bit her lip as the memories playing on the edge of her consciousness began to tell a story. Monday, standing in front of the jaguars' cage, John Winston had told Matt that he hadn't been to Jacky's ranch in years. Yet yesterday in Cohen's office, he had asked if the cage had been found in the unfinished section of the barn. He would have said "unfinished section" only if he had been there, Lisa thought, and seen for himself what the area under construction looked like. The renovation of the barn had begun only a couple of months ago. Therefore, Winston must have been there recently. He must have been there Monday afternoon

171

when he murdered Tony and put cocaine in the cage as part of his plan to implicate Koo in Jacky's murder.

Lisa remembered something else. It was John Winston who prevented Matt from going to the ranch on Monday by giving him a job—a trumped-up job—that Matt thought he was being given because of Winston's disapproval of the way he had handled the zoo's finances. What Winston was really after was to stall them for a day to give him time to take care of things.

So, Matt's fear that his interest in the cages had triggered Tony's murder was, in part, warranted. John Winston had listened to Matt and conceived of the idea of making Matt's hunch about the cages come true, not only to draw suspicion away from himself, but to implicate Koo as the murderer. Winston hated Koo and wanted to get rid of him because he was Johnny's lover. And in trying to convince the police that Koo was guilty of Jacky's murder, he must have convinced Johnny.

"Oh, Johnny, if only you had waited," Lisa whispered. The tragedy was large enough. It hadn't needed amplifying. It was all crystal clear to her now. Wearily, she got out of the chair and continued her search for the key. She was looking through the odds and ends in the top drawer on the off-chance that Johnny had simply thrown the key in among the paper clips and boxes of staples, when she heard the soft click of the door opening. She whirled around and faced the man standing in the doorway, his lips curved into a tight smile.

26

JOHN WINSTON was dressed casually in dark slacks and a sweater. But there was nothing casual about the gun he held in his hand. It was pointed at Lisa's heart.

Lisa slammed the drawer closed as if by this action she could hide what she was doing in Johnny's office.

"I believe I have what you're looking for," Winston said, holding up a key in his left hand while he trained the gun on her with his right.

"What?" Lisa asked, stalling for time, but knowing he knew exactly what she was doing.

"You want to play games, do you?"

"I don't know what you're . . ." she began, but he cut her off.

"Do exactly as you're told," he said. "And don't give me any trouble or I'll kill you right here."

Lisa's breath caught in her throat. He meant it. She could tell he did. She froze, her hands still on the drawer handle.

He walked toward her. Always watching her, he knelt down beside her and opened the bottom right-hand drawer of Johnny's desk, as if he knew exactly what he would find there. He took out the jeans and boots and put them into a plastic shopping bag looped over his left elbow. Then he took

Lisa's arm and pressed the hard nose of the gun against her side.

"All right, we'll take a little walk now. Light our way with your flashlight."

They left the office, as close as lovers, and he hurried her along the corridor, pulling her past Matt's office toward the rear of the building.

Lisa was filled with despair. They passed the restrooms and reached the back door. Winston opened it and pushed her out ahead of him. Outside in the cold starry night, she felt a sudden rush of hope.

"Don't even think of it," he said, reading her thoughts.

Lisa considered screaming. How much of a sound could she get out before he pulled the trigger, ending her sound forever? In any case, there was no one here to hear her, no one human, anyway. He had killed twice. What would prevent him from killing again? No one but the exotic animals would know until her body was discovered in the morning. Probably by Matt on his rounds, as he had discovered Jacky's body. She thought of Matt, sleeping peacefully in his armchair. He'd wake up. He'd see the note and notice his keys and gate card were missing. He'd know she was here. Would he come to the zoo to look for her?

Now they were walking fast, toward the tiger enclosure. In the moonlight she could see the little pond catching silver like a coin and the trees silhouetted against the moonlit sky. And beyond the pond, near the Big Cats House, the tigers lay silent. Were they inside or out tonight? Were they sleeping or awake? She thought she saw their dark forms on the grass, but it might have been only tree shadows moving in the breeze.

"You killed Jacky, didn't you," she said, "and then you killed Tony, just to throw us off the track."

"If you say so."

"Johnny thinks Koo was Jacky's murderer, doesn't he?"

Winston gave a little laugh. "Yes. Johnny's heart is broken that his 'mom' is dead and he's sure Koo did it. I wish he hadn't killed him, though."

"You were the one who convinced Johnny that Koo was Jacky's killer, weren't you?"

"I did. And I knew Johnny wanted to avenge her death, but I never thought he'd kill Koo."

"And he knows that you're here tonight, right?"

"Oh, I see what you're driving at. It's true he knows I've come here to collect his clothes, the evidence that he was inside the tiger enclosure. But he won't know that I met you, quite by chance, rummaging through his drawers."

"Why did you kill her? Because she was planning to leave you?"

"Not at all. It was an accident. I didn't mean to kill her. I always cared about her."

"Then why?"

"She did something that made me very angry. I lost my temper and hit her. She fell against the corner of the mantelpiece in our bedroom, hit her head and died."

"It was an accident?"

"An accident. But in retrospect, not such an unfortunate one for me."

"I see."

"No, you don't. She'd been snooping. Stupidly, I'd once bragged to her about outfoxing the government. She looked through my papers until she found that I hadn't declared some large fees that I believed would never be noticed by the IRS. She threatened to expose me if I didn't give her a divorce and a rather large settlement."

"And exposure would've meant prison for you?"

"Possibly, or I might have just been fined. But my reputation in the community would have suffered. It was knowing

175

that she would want to hurt me after all my generosity to her that made me so angry. But I didn't intend to kill her."

"So she died in your home and then you dumped her into the polar bear's cage."

Lisa suddenly remembered something. "And the shoes. You put her sandals on her feet, didn't you."

"A mistake," Winston admitted.

"What's Johnny going to think when he begins to figure out some of this?"

"He won't," Winston said tightly. "But in any case, he's in no position to protest. I'm protecting him from a murder rap."

They were now on the gravel path heading toward the gate to the tiger enclosure, the very spot where she had smelled the ammonia early this morning. She felt a weakness beginning in her ankles that made her knees shake uncontrollably.

He must have felt her pull back, for he held her tightly as he turned the key in the lock of the gate. "We'll leave your pocketbook here, just outside the gate. They'll say, 'She climbed in, stupid little busybody, and couldn't climb out again.' "

"No." She tried to pull back.

At the sound of her voice there was a low growl. A tiger. She could see its form, dark on the grass in front of its sleeping quarters. It lifted its head and flicked sensitive ears, then with a snuffle like a snore put its head back down.

———————————⊃ ⊂——————

Matt turned into the lot, his tires screaming on loose gravel. He parked next to Lisa's old VW beside the gate, let himself into the zoo, and ran to the administration building. Inside, the corridor was dark and silent. He ran by the door to

Johnny's office. He opened his office door. "Lisa. Lisa," he called as he turned on the light.

He stood in the middle of the room thinking. Where would she have gone? What had she been talking about before he fell asleep? He thought hard. Koo. She'd been talking about Koo. She'd been talking about the cage that opened so mysteriously allowing the tiger to get at him. The Big Cats House. She must have gone there to check out some idea.

He raced along the corridor to the back door and turned left on the path to the Big Cats House.

"Silence is your best defense," Winston whispered as he opened the gate and stepped into the enclosure, dragging Lisa along with him. He locked the gate behind them. He let go of her arm, and with the gun aimed at her at close range, he pulled a bottle out of his pocket and squirted ammonia all around himself. Then he grabbed her arm again.

The ammonia vapors were so strong that Lisa could hardly breathe as he pulled her along beside the fence until they reached the gate on the far side of the enclosure that faced Route 63.

He let go of her again, unlocked the gate, opened the door slightly and started to slide through. Fear gave Lisa strength. She struggled against him and fought to get out the door with him. He pushed her away with his gun hand. The hard metal slammed into her stomach and she fell backward, but she hung onto his arm.

He fell with her. Then, righting himself, he unclenched her hand and threw her into the enclosure. She landed on her back on the grass and dirt, but jumped up as the door clanged shut.

At the sound of the door, the low growl started up again.

177

Lisa tried to open the gate but she was too late. Winston turned the key in the lock. He stood there on the outside and smiled as she shook the gate.

"Wait."

He put a finger to his lips. "Shh. Maybe you'll live a little longer if you're nice and quiet." He turned away.

"Don't leave me here. The police will figure it out. They'll put it all together, just as I did."

Winston walked away.

Alone, Lisa stood with her back to the fence, watching the tigers. Then she turned to the fence. She tried to brace the tip of one boot against it, but she couldn't get a foothold.

"Damn, damn," she muttered. She studied the fence. She could get handholds on the chain-link fence, but she couldn't climb that way.

She turned back and looked at the tigers. One of them was already beginning to move. She watched it flatten itself to the ground in a huge stretch. Slowly the tiger got to its feet, still stretching, head down, forelegs straight. Then it stood still, frozen in place, and turned its head toward Lisa. For a moment they stared at each other across the field. Then the tiger started to move. Slowly. And she heard a low theatening growl that filled her ears like thunder.

The tiger was coming, not running as if it were tracking prey, but walking carefully. For a moment it was lost from view as it passed into the heavy shadows of a tree. Lisa strained her eyes to see where it would reappear. Her breathing was fast and shallow. She felt faint. She thought of an alley cat she had watched playing with a mouse. It would strike the mouse with its paw and then sit back to wait until the victim moved again. One little twitch and the cat would strike the mouse again, sink its teeth into the soft flesh until the mouse lay still, finally, a tiny mat of grayish fur puddled in blood. Then the cat lost interest. Lisa wished she understood more about how tigers behave. Should she shout, jump around, try to scare it away? Or had Winston been correct when he told her silence was her best defense?

Suddenly the big cat reappeared, gliding out of the shadows. It had covered about half the distance between them and it was moving steadily toward her. Every muscle, every sense was alert. It growled again, the sound like a snarl. It was walking faster. Its eyes were amber discs, glowing in the dark, steadily upon her. If only he will just kill me right off, Lisa prayed. She thought of the agonies of the dying mouse.

The Big Cats House was dark, lighted only by the globe above the entrance. Matt hurried in. "Lisa," he called. "Are you here? Lisa?"

The jaguars' eyes glowed like four circles of yellow light as they watched Matt moving around the exhibit area. Matt heard a growl from one of the sleeping areas behind the cages. He could see nothing out of the ordinary. He looked through his keys for the one that would unlock the door to Tom O'Rourke's office.

The tiger was about twenty feet away now. Its fur glowed in moonlight. Lisa could see the markings on its face. A smell nudged at her consciousness. She reached into her pocket. She took out the bottle she'd taken from Johnny's drawer and pressed down on the button. A spray of liquid squirted out and made her cough. Her eyes were watering so much that she could hardly see the tiger. Then she saw that he had stopped. He stood stiffly, ears straight up. She could see the look of concentration on his face. He sniffed.

Hope flared up. Oh, please make this work, she prayed.

The tiger was moving again, coming toward her, but more slowly. Even in her terror she recognized the beauty of the animal, the cool power and symmetry of its movements. She sprayed again, all around herself. The smell was nearly intolerable. The ammonia vapor filled her eyes. Her mouth and nostrils stung from it. She squirted again, a long hard blast toward the tiger, who was now only about ten feet away.

She pressed down on the button again and, to her horror, nothing came out of the nozzle. She shook the bottle. No liquid sloshed around inside. Empty. The tiger, coughing and spluttering, turned and ran away.

Lisa continued to cough. She wiped her eyes on her sleeve. She thrust the useless bottle back into her pocket. The tiger was standing next to its mate, looking in her direction. The other tiger that had been sleeping was stirring. In a matter of moments the second tiger would catch Lisa's scent and come bounding over to investigate. Maybe the ammonia would disguise her scent for a while, but it couldn't last long.

Already breezes were dispersing the odor. Lisa got an acid whiff of tiger urine as the wind whipped her hair across her face. It could only be a few more minutes before both tigers came over to her, and this time, she had no way to save herself.

Unless . . . She looked up at the fence again. It seemed about twelve feet high with barbed wire across the top. She pulled off her boots and threw them on the ground, then her socks.

In her bare feet she tried for a toehold in the links of the fence. Almost. She bent her big toes, fitting them to the open spaces in the mesh. Thank God she had inherited Anna's long elegant big toes. It hurt to put her weight on them, but she thought about how much more the tigers' claws and teeth would hurt. She grabbed onto the links with her fingers and began to pull herself up the fence.

She took one tentative step, then another. Her arms ached. She climbed slowly. Too slowly, she realized, as she dared a glance in the direction of the tigers. Both of them stood looking at her.

She was, she realized, a moving target in the moonlight. The just-awakened tiger was watching her with a cat-to-mouse concentration. Then it began to move toward her, much faster than the other tiger had. Its mate followed.

She was now about halfway up the fence. The tigers could easily reach up and pull her down. She could almost picture them up on their hind legs, their forepaws reaching up, grabbing her in their sharp claws and pulling her down to the ground.

———

Matt switched on the overhead light in Tom's office. The office was messy, the desk cluttered with papers. He saw no sign that Lisa had been there. He opened the top desk drawer. The keys to the cage control box were there, just where they were supposed to be. The police had examined them and returned them. Somehow, Matt had thought that Lisa might have wanted to look at them. Apparently not. What had she wanted here at the zoo? Where the hell was she? He left the Big Cats House and began to run up the path toward the Bear Dens.

———

Lisa concentrated on climbing. Faster than she'd ever have imagined possible, she lifted one foot up after the other, finding toeholds that were exactly that, openings in the mesh just large enough for her toes.

Her arms ached, her toes were bruised. She paid no attention to pain, thinking of that greater pain she must escape, thinking of death. "I don't want to die. I don't," she whispered softly to herself, spurring herself on, fighting the limitations of her body, fighting her terror.

The tigers were almost at the fence. Lisa made a last huge effort and pulled herself up until her hands were just below the strands of barbed wire placed across the top of the fence so that humans could not perform this feat that she must perform.

The tigers were at the bottom of the fence, looking up at her. Two pairs of golden eyes reflecting light. They were snarling. The larger one leaped against the fence, its claws glistened in moonlight. It came dangerously close to her bare foot before it fell down.

Carefully, she took the last step. At the very top of the fence she wrapped her scarf around her right hand and, holding down the top strand of barbed wire, she lifted her legs over the top.

Her jeans caught on the barbs and she heard the ripping sound as they tore, the barb cutting into her leg. Now she had one leg over the top. She brought the other leg over, still holding onto the wire with her scarf-wrapped hand.

She panted with exhaustion and relief. Down below the tigers were looking up and snarling angrily, deprived of a midnight snack.

If she climbed down on the other side, they might be able to claw her through the fence. She took a few steps down. Below, the grass was deep and matted. Carefully she let go with her right hand and toe, then pushed off and jumped. She fell forward into the grass, breaking her fall with her hands.

Inside the tiger enclosure the two big cats were following her every move with their intense hunting expression, leaping against the fence. Still shaking, Lisa stood up and checked for damage. She was bruised and cut from the barbed wire. And she had one more fence to go. But everything seemed intact.

Safe from the tigers, her fear instantly shifted to Winston. It was certainly possible that he would come back to make sure the tigers had done their work. He couldn't afford to have her live. Therefore, she couldn't afford to rest. She began to climb the second fence.

Matt was sweating and out of breath as he raced back down the road from the Bear Dens toward the Administration Building. He'd call Cohen, ask him to come out here right away with some men to help him find Lisa. He couldn't imagine where she could be, what she was up to. He was running by the tiger enclosure, when he saw it. He stopped. He leaned against the fence and looked more closely. On the fence at the far end of the enclosure, something was moving. A figure. He could see it silhouetted against the highway lights. Matt veered around and raced back to the parking lot. He got in his car and headed for Route 63.

It seemed to take forever to climb the second fence. Lisa was truly exhausted now. Her right toe was so sore, she thought it might be broken. But her fear drove her on. And finally she managed to climb up one side and down the other of the second fence.

She lay on the grass by the side of the road for only a few moments to catch her breath. She heard a car drive up and stop near her. She pulled herself up. She'd begun to move toward the bushes, half-crawling, looking for a place to hide, when she heard Matt's voice. "Lisa. For God's sake. What are you doing?"

27

THE YOUNG OFFICER at the desk at Braeton Police Head-quarters looked like a high school kid. Matt held Lisa's arm as they walked up to the desk. She looked, she knew, like something the cat had dragged in. In this case, the cliché was almost too apt.

"Call Lieutenant Cohen," she said as Matt helped her into a chair beside the desk.

"I'm not authorized to do that," the young officer replied.

They waited until he called in his superior, a tired-looking sergeant with bags under his eyes and a rumpled uniform. Together, Lisa and Matt managed to convince him of the seriousness of the matter.

In Sergeant Longo's office, he handed her the telephone and Lisa briefly told Cohen her story.

Then they waited. Sergeant Longo brought coffee. Matt helped Lisa clean and bandage her cuts.

Cohen arrived twenty minutes later with a handcuffed John Winston. "He had these with him," he said, holding up Johnny's clothes in the plastic bag. He was shaking his head in disbelief at the stupidity of it.

Winston started to speak, but Cohen interrupted. "Let me read you your rights, before you say anything."

After Cohen read him his rights, Winston seemed to collapse in a heap, all the arrogant fizzle gone out of him. Lisa didn't feel sorry for him.

Soon Johnny was brought in. Hughes and another policeman were on either side of him. They seemed to be holding him up. Cohen read him his rights immediately, but Johnny hardly listened. "Koo did it," he said. "He killed her. He killed Jacky."

"What makes you think Koo killed your stepmother?" Cohen asked.

"He did," Johnny insisted. "My father said . . . I told my father about Koo's being jailed for dealing. My father said Koo helped her bring the cage up to the ranch. So I knew Koo did it."

"How did you know about the drugs?"

"Jacky. She was warning me about him. The night she was killed. She should've taken the warning herself."

Cohen looked out past Johnny. "Koo didn't kill her."

"Who did?"

No one answered him.

"Who?" he asked again, trying for control.

At last he noticed his father. Noticed the cuffs. "You." Johnny ran at his father. Cohen caught him, held him back.

"It was an accident," Winston said, his voice weak.

"You made me think . . ." Johnny couldn't say anymore.
"I never thought you'd . . ."

"How did you get the key to the tiger enclosure?" Cohen broke in.

"I got the combination to the safe. I knew my father had written it in the back of his diary. When I found out she was dead, I sneaked the key out and had it duplicated."

"Why?"

"So I could put the heel near the fence, so you wouldn't keep looking for it."

185

"Why did you want to do that?"

Johnny had his face in his hands. "I was scared. We'd had an argument that night in a bar. People heard. I walked out, mad. I thought . . . I thought you'd think it was me killed her. See, later I came back for her. That's when she told me about Koo's drug conviction. She wanted to warn me so I wouldn't let him move in with me." Johnny began to sob, then got himself under control. "That's when her heel broke off, when I was driving her home. She looked in my car for it, but couldn't find it. Later, after I heard she'd been killed, I found the heel. In my car. I was scared you'd think I killed her. So I had the key duplicated and waited for a chance to put it near the fence."

"Obstructing justice. Minor, compared to the rest." Cohen looked tired and not happy.

John Winston was a changed man from the man Lisa had heard speak with such confidence at the zoo Gala. He looked shrunken, his face pale, even his walk had changed.

Father and son stood looking at each other without speaking.

"I didn't mean to kill her," Winston said.

"She was just an object to you. To be used as needed," Johnny's voice had lost all expression. "Like all of us."

"No. That's not true. I love you. You're my son. Once I loved her."

Johnny was shaking his head. "Love. You don't know love from horse shit. You ruined everything you touched. You killed my mother. . . ." Winston started to protest, but Johnny outshouted him. "Yes, you killed her. You must have made her so miserable she drank and used her car as a weapon against herself. And now Jacky too." He laughed helplessly. "And I got rid of Koo for you. Oh, but you wouldn't have killed him, would you? You needed him to take the rap."

"I was trying to help you get away from him."

186

Johnny turned to Cohen. "Put me in a cell," he said, "far away from him."

Cohen nodded and two policemen led Johnny away. He didn't look back.

"I want to call my lawyer," Winston said, beginning to pull himself together. "I'm afraid I've said too much."

Cohen nodded to Hughes. "Take him to the phone outside."

"Not very pretty," Cohen said to Lisa when they'd gone, "Ms. Davis," he added with a grin.

Lisa knew he was trying to cheer her up. "No, Lieutenant Cohen," she said, but couldn't manage a smile. "What will happen to Johnny?"

"He killed a man. Premeditated too."

"I know. But he seems to be so easily manipulated."

"In our justice system it's knowing the difference between right and wrong that matters, not manipulability."

Lisa nodded. A wave of exhaustion took her by surprise.

Cohen smiled again, this time for real. "I leave you in good hands, Ms. Davis," he said as he sat down at his desk. To Matt he said, "Take her home. She's had quite a night."

Lisa was at her desk at the *Times* the next day finishing her story on the zoo murders when Matt called.

"I got a package in the mail today. From Adam Klinger, you know, the guy who's taking care of the ranch. It's Jacky's breeding log. It explains what she was doing with the cages. It explains a lot."

"Tell me."

"The day after the jags arrived, she and Koo brought Dakar, the zoo's male cheetah, up to her ranch and mated him with her cheetah, who was in estrus. She recorded it in her breeding log."

"So that's why one cage was at the ranch and one at the zoo. She must've brought both cages to the ranch that Wednesday, then brought one back to the zoo when she returned Dakar."

"I think that's right. And another thing. It explains the coincidence of Tom O'Rourke being away on that Wednesday."

"How does it explain that?"

"Because it was no coincidence. She and Koo couldn't have taken Dakar from the zoo if Tom was there. He wouldn't have let them."

"Why not?"

"He's a stickler for the rules."

"She could've asked you."

Matt was silent. When he spoke, his voice was husky. "She didn't want to ask me. She wanted to surprise me. If the mating took, she was going to give me one of the cubs. She says so in the log."

"Oh, Matt."

They were both quiet.

Then Lisa said, "Well, that ties it up, I guess. All the loose ends."

"The loose ends. All tied up."

Lisa heard the sorrow in his voice and didn't know what to say. She looked down at the story she was shaping, the story about the zoo murders. "I think she really cared about you," she said.

"Yes."

Lisa didn't know whether that made him feel better or worse right now. But someday, she knew, he would feel better, knowing that Jacky had loved him, in her own way.